ROCK A BYE BABY

WILLOW ROSE

Cover design by Jan Sigetty Boeje
https://www.facebook.com/pages/Sigettys Cover Design

Special thanks to my editor Jean Pacillo
http://www.ebookeditingpro.com

———

To be the first to hear about new releases and bargains from Willow Rose. Sign up to be on the VIP list below.

I promise not to share your email with anyone else, and I won't clutter your inbox.

- SIGN UP TO BE ON THE VIP LIST HERE :
http://eepurl.com/wcGej

Connect with Willow Rose:

willow-rose.net

CHAPTER ONE

I'M DOING my Zumba class. I'm sweating heavily while glancing anxiously at the baby carriage on the other side of the window where my princess is sleeping heavily next to all the other babies who have come with their mommies to the *Mommy-and-Me Zumba Extraordinaire* that the local fitness center in Karrebaeksminde hosts every Monday morning. Monday, naturally, because they know Monday is the day every mom wants to start a new life of exercise and diet. The carriage is not moving. She's still asleep I think relieved while I push myself and dance to the fast rhythms trying hard to sweat off the butt giving birth to my third child has given me.

I'm forty-one, I'm not tired as my mother says I am. I have enough energy to do it all. I know I do.

When I come home, the baby is still sleeping. I eat an organic, low-carb, fat-reduced lunch and drink a smoothie made from beet, spinach, lemon and apple. I drink a skinny-latte afterwards while reading the *Zeeland Times*. My old friend from high school Rebekka Franck has an article in the paper about a fire in Neastved, the biggest city close to us. I read it feeling good, happy and energized from the exercise and healthy food. I detect a typo in the third line of the article. It annoys me. I pick up my iPhone and call the newspaper to let them know. They tell me that they are very sorry, and that they'll make sure to tell whoever is responsible. I hang up feeling good about myself. If people make a mistake they need to know.

The baby is making sounds, I pick her up and bring her to the changing table. Quiet, cleanliness and regularity those are the keywords to having a baby. I change the diaper and tickle her stomach. Josephine is three months old. I gave birth to her on a Sunday after only three hours of labor. I had a natural birth. No sedatives. Just me and nature. I gave birth in water in my own house. The mid-wife came to help, but I didn't need her much. I didn't even need my husband. Like the two first times I did it by myself. I took control of the birth. It's my body, I told them when they wanted to discuss anesthesia. I told them I found it repulsive that they wanted to sedate me, I told them that women through all times, in all kinds of countries had done this without being sedated, so why shouldn't I?

I am not a natural blond, but I do color it which I'll admit to if asked, but I won't reveal that I recently had a laser-treatment remove the facial hair that is beginning to grow on my chin and upper lip.

My baby is laughing and smiling, but all I see is the weird blemish in her forehead that won't go away. Strawberry mark, the mid-wife had told me after the baby had arrived and I saw the mark. "It'll eventually disappear on its own." But it hadn't. Not yet. I'm thinking tumor and look it up on the Internet while the baby is in the playpen. An article suggests that scientists don't agree on the subject. In some babies they even keep growing, some parents have them frozen and cut off when the baby is six months old. I consider it. I look up doctors who will do that for me and write their names down. I put the note on top of the other notes, I've made the last week.

I get up and walk to the kitchen. I drink a glass of water, one of eight I have decided to drink every day to make sure I get enough water. The baby is whining, I pick her up and give her my breast. I read a magazine about educating children while my baby drinks her milk. I have breastfed all of my kids till they were more than a year as is recommended by the Danish health department. *To give your baby the best start*, the flyer from the hospital said.

I read about sibling jealousy and decide to spend more time with my older children when they come home from school. I think about my husband and plan to give him a blow-job tonight after reading another article about the difficulties relationships experience once there is a new baby in the house. It's been three weeks since we last had sex, I count by looking in my calendar in the phone where I have marked the last time. It's about time we get intimate for the sake of our marriage.

The baby sucks on my breast and it hurts slightly. Such a precious time, I think to myself. And so brief, when they're all dependent on you and your breasts. I caress my princess' thin hair while I sing to her.

Rock-a-bye baby, on the treetop,
When the wind blows, the cradle will rock,
When the bough breaks, the cradle will fall,
And down will come baby, cradle and all.

CHAPTER TWO

MY OLDEST daughter is the first to come home. I have just put the baby down for her afternoon nap when I hear the front door open. I jump down the stairs and welcome her as she enters.

"How was your day, sweetie?" I ask.

Amalie throws her bag in the hallway and her jacket on top of it. She gives me a look, walks past me to the kitchen while grumbling "Whatever."

I pick her jacket up from the floor and put it on a hanger. I brush it off lightly and remove a couple of spots with my nail, scratching them off before I put it in the closet. I place her backpack by the foot of the stairs so she can grab it before she runs upstairs to do her homework. I hear her go through the refrigerator and feel my hands shake lightly at the thought of the mess she is about to make. I calm myself down by counting to ten a few times before I brace myself and walk over to her.

"Any news from school?" I ask keeping my smile on even when everything inside of me frozen by the look of the counter where she is now making herself a sandwich.

She looks at me like I'm a complete idiot.

"Like what?"

I shrug and try to not let the tone in her voice bother me. I close the refrigerator door and stand by the sink. "So there's nothing new to tell me? Any cute guys we should talk about?"

Amalie rolls her eyes at me and sighs frustrated. "Please don't pretend to be interested in my life, Mom. It's gross."

"How can it be gross?"

She sighs again. "It just is. It's too much all of a sudden."

I tilt my head. "All of a sudden? I've always been interested in your life. You know that."

Amalie scoffs. "As if ..."

"What do you mean?"

"Ah come on. You and Daddy haven't been the least bit interested in me and Jacob ever since ..." Amalie pauses and looks at me. Then she shakes her head. "Never mind."

"Ever since what exactly, Amalie?" I ask. "Since I had the baby?"

Amalie shrugs. "Yeah. You know. Whatever."

I nod and smile to let her know I understand and respect her feelings just like the article told me to do. Jealousy was common in the older children and could be very difficult for them to express. It is my job as a mother to help them put words to their feelings.

"So what you're saying is I don't pay you and your brother enough attention. Is that it?" I say to help her find the words.

Amalie shrugs again. "Well, I mean it's only natural that you don't, with all that has been going on and all. It's just ... well it's been three months now and ... well I guess I'm wondering how long this is going to keep on?"

I nod again understandingly. "I know sweetie. It must have been hard on the two of you."

Amalie nods slowly. "Yeah. It kind of has been. I mean with everything going on at home and all, it's been pretty hard to focus on school. So ... I guess what I'm saying is ..." Amalie looks into my eyes, then hesitates. "You know what? I'll just talk to Dad about it."

"You can tell me anything, Amalie. You know that," I say. "I'm here for you."

"Are you sure you can handle it?"

I smile at my daughter's great compassion for me. Worry about me just because I haven't been sleeping much lately. Yes I am tired from being up several times at night and breastfeeding, but I can certainly find the strength to listen to my daughter's problems. "I'm stronger than I seem," I say.

"Well ... It seems I might be ... failing math."

I feel my fingers grow numb. My daughter reads it on my face.

"My teacher says it's okay. I can take a summer class and there will be no problem after that. It's okay, mom. It really is."

I restrain myself, but my nostrils won't relax, neither will the vein in my forehead that my daughter is now staring at.

"Mom? Are you okay?" she asks.

I close my eyes and count to ten, then count again and force pictures of relaxing places, long, white beaches stretching as far as the eye can see, nice clean hotels with nice service and rose petals on the nicely made bed. I open my eyes again and look at my daughter. Then I reach out and touch her cheek gently. "Of course I'm okay," I say. "Now what did you say the name of your teacher was?"

CHAPTER THREE

I GO directly to the front office and ask to speak with Mr. Berendsen, my daughter's math teacher. They tell me he has gone home for the day but will be back tomorrow. I smile and nod politely, then leave the high school, running down the street pushing my sleeping baby in the carriage in front of me.

I know where he lives. It's right next to the school, so I decide to leave the car by the school. A few seconds later I'm by his door. I park the baby carriage in his yard, then walk to the window and look in. I spot Mr. Berendsen inside his kitchen preparing dinner. He's alone. I bang on the window. Mr. Berendsen jumps inside of the house. I am grinning as he spots me. I point at the door. He hesitates, then walks towards it. He opens it slightly.

"Yes? Can I help you with anything?" he asks.

"As a matter of fact, I believe you can," I say and walk closer. He seems afraid of me. "You're my daughter's teacher. Amalie Rasmussen?"

Mr. Berendsen relaxes and opens the door further. "Ah, Amalie. In three a?"

"Yes, that's her. I'm her mother. My name is Lisa," I say and we shake hands. Mr. Berendsen seems more relaxed now and he invites me inside. I accept and follow him into the kitchen.

"I'm in the middle of preparing dinner, so if you won't mind I'll be continuing while we talk."

"Having company over?" I ask and sit at a kitchen chair.

"No, just for myself. I'm alone. I have been ever since the wife left me two years ago."

I nod and smile like I know how that feels, which I don't, cause I have never been divorced. I would never let that happen to me.

"So what happened?" I ask.

"What do you mean?"

"Why did your wife leave you?"

Mr. Berendsen seems startled by the question, but I pretend I don't notice. I look around the small kitchen and spot dust and dog hairs in the corner. I pick some up, thinking this house needs cleaning. It annoys me that people live like this. Filthy. Disgusting. Lazy. I look to see if I can locate the dog.

"Why?" he asks.

"Why what?"

"Why do you want to know that?"

I shrug with a smile. "Just curious." I pause and look at the man while he is chopping carrots. "Maybe you cheated on her?"

The knife slips in Mr. Berendsen's hand and he almost cuts himself. I look at him awaiting my answer.

"You are extraordinarily direct," he says. "But if you must know then yes, I had an affair, but only briefly. She had one that lasted for several years and now she is living with him." He goes back to chopping carrots.

"I thought it would be something like that," I say.

Mr. Berendsen stops chopping again and looks at me. "Why?" he asks.

"Why what?"

"Why did you think it might be *something like that?*" he asks gesticulating wildly with the knife in his hand making quotation signs.

"Be careful," I say. "Don't cut yourself."

Mr. Berendsen calms down and puts the knife on the table. Then he sighs and looks at me. "Tell me again, why did you come here?"

"Oh. It was about my daughter," I say. "She tells me you're failing her."

"Well she's the one failing the class. She's been very unfocused lately and hasn't done well on the tests. I'm sorry, but I have to fail her. I told her she could take a summer class to make up for it."

"Yes. I heard that. But you see there is the problem that we're planning on going to Paris all summer, to visit an old friend of mine who lives outside the city in a big wine-castle and who has children the same age. We've had this all planned out and now ... well we can't just change something that has already been planned, now can we? You see my problem, Mr. Berendsen?"

"It's just for a week. If she passes the test, she'll be fine. You'll still be able to go to France for several weeks."

I slam my clenched fist onto the table. Mr. Berendsen jumps. "Exactly how many weeks we have isn't the problem here, Mr. Berendsen. It's the fact that we have to CHANGE our plans, that you force us to rearrange everything just for you, just to make you happy. This is what is wrong with this world today. NO one respects anything or anyone any more, everything is just me, me and me. It's all about what I can get out of it and someone simply has to put a stopper for this behavior, don't you think Mr. Berendsen? I mean how are the young people to learn how to respect other people's plans if all they see is that we can just CHANGE it to fit everyone's need and do whatever they lust after whenever they lust for it. Not everything in life is like a marriage that you can just CHANGE and throw away like you want to, Mr. Berendsen. Some things have to be steady in life; some things just can't be CHANGED!"

I am standing up now, without even realizing it. Mr. Berendsen is staring at me. I close my eyes for a second while pressing my gloved hands against each other. When I open my eyes again, I'm smiling at him. "So you must understand that you need to let my daughter pass. Do we understand each other? I think we do."

"Mrs. Rasmussen. I simply can't let your daughter pass this class just because you've planned a trip to France this summer."

I walk closer to him. He holds the knife out in front of him. I can tell he's afraid of me. "You can't or you won't?" I ask.

He never answers. I'm thinking tenderloin for dinner tonight.

CHAPTER FOUR

THE BABY keeps me awake almost all night and I attend to her, sit in the nursery and rock her in the rocking chair while singing softly to her. It helps her calm down, but she doesn't fall asleep. When the sun comes up I'm too tired to get up and I ask Christian to take care of the older kids, to make their lunches and drive them to school. He does so without arguing. I tell myself I should give him that blow-job soon, since I was too tired last night. The baby is finally sleeping, and I try to get some rest, but it's too bright outside for me to fall asleep. I stay in bed and listen while the house becomes quiet. After that I feel restless and take a shower.

I walk downstairs and pick up the paper. I read it while sipping my skinny-latte and gulping down a smoothie made from raspberries, rice milk, honey, ginger, flaxseed and lemon juice. Rebekka Franck has a story in the paper about a man who had acid thrown in his face in an accident at work and is now in the hospital. I find a grammatical error almost at the end of the article and call the newspaper to let them know. The lady answering tells me she can't see what it is, but tells me she will let whoever is responsible know. I hang up. I drink the rest of my smoothie and go to the bathroom. The baby is still sleeping. I should get some sleep too, but can't seem to rest. The house is dirty and needs to be cleaned. I can't seem to relax when the house is filthy. So I clean it. I wash the windows, mop the floors and polish the silverware I inherited from my grandmother when she died. I think I can still smell her sickness on it. I rub it again and again trying to get the smell off, but without success. I still feel restless when the house is cleaned. I think I need to get out of the house, so I grab the baby and put her in the carriage without waking her. I go for a stroll in the city and feel better. I walk through a park where I meet other mothers. They smile at me and I smile back. Children are playing at the playground, but I am afraid they're going to wake up my princess, so I keep walking. My mother calls me and asks me out for lunch. We meet at a café and have a salad. I don't eat the croutons or the bread that comes with it to not get too many carbs. The chicken tastes good but a little dry.

"Your dad and I went to the opera last night," she says. "They play *Il Trittico* these days. It's splendid. You and Christian should go soon. Get out a little you know. It would do you good."

I nod while chewing. Discreetly she lets me know I have something on my lip. I wipe it off with my napkin.

"We had dinner at Restaurant Bojesen just before we went. It wasn't Noma, I tell you that," she laughs. "At least it was better than this," she continues. "I mean what have they done to this poor chicken?"

I don't answer. I focus on my food and glance at the baby carriage outside. Josephine is still sleeping. I'm thinking about dinner tonight. I'm torn between spaghetti Bolognese or an oven dish with my special sauce. I can't seem to decide.

"Have you done something with your hair?" my mother asks. "You really should. I have the best new hairdresser. He's in Copenhagen, but I don't mind the drive. He's the best. Did the crown-princess' hair before she married the prince. Oh, he's excellent. Can't you tell?"

I nod even if I didn't hear half of what she said. My eyes are fixated on a woman and a man sitting in the corner of the café. They're fighting over something. She is crying but tries to hide it so no one will see. They have a child with them. He's fussing, he doesn't like them arguing. He is no more than two, I guess. He wants out of his high chair, his mother helps him, still while arguing with the man. The boy is now on the floor. He takes off. Stumbles across the room and starts to bother people. They all smile. He stops at one table where two women are eating. He puts his fingers in their food throws it across the room. He hits someone in the neck. The parents don't notice. They're still fighting. My mother goes on and on about their trip to Vietnam last month. I pretend to be listening, but can't get my eyes off the child who is now terrorizing another couple. The mother finally notices and rushes after him. She slaps him across the face and everyone in the café gasps. Then she takes him by the hand and drags him crying out of the café. I close my eyes and start counting. My mother's mouth is still moving when I open them again. I put down my fork on the plate. I get up. My mother stops talking.

"Where are you going?" she asks.

"I lost my appetite," I say.

I leave. I grab the baby carriage and run after the couple down the street. They're still fighting and the kid is crying. I walk right behind them. They don't notice me. Still fighting they walk into an alley pushing the child in a stroller in front of them. I follow them. Now they see me and stop and look at me.

"What do you want?" the man asks.

"Don't you know it's wrong to hit a child?" I ask. "It's actually illegal in this country."

The man steps forward with a menacing look. "What did you say?" he asks.

I stare into his eyes then repeat it. "It's wrong to hit a child."

He doesn't seem to understand and it annoys me. It troubles me that people that stupid are allowed to even have a child.

He looks at me like he wants to slap me. I can tell he has been hitting his girlfriend by the look of the bruises on her face.

"I give you three seconds to get the hell out of here, before I beat the crap out of you," he says.

I don't move.

CHAPTER FIVE

A MALIE IS at home when I get back. Josephine is awake and I place her in the playpen after changing her.

"You're home early?" I ask when I get out into the kitchen where she is eating her sandwich leaving a mess I know I eventually have to clean up.

Amalie smiles for the first time in weeks. "Math was cancelled today."

"Really? How come?"

Amalie shrugs. "I don't know. I guess Mr. Berendsen was sick or something."

"But they didn't send a substitute? They usually do?"

"Yeah," she says while chewing with her mouth open. "It's weird. It was like no one knew he wasn't there. We waited in class for him for twenty minutes, when he still didn't come someone went to the front office to ask what was going on. They said they hadn't heard from him. He only had one class today. Maybe he forgot?"

I take an apple and wash it before I bite it. It's juicy but firm, just the way I like it. I chew while thinking. "It sure doesn't sound like him," I say.

Amalie shrugs. "Nah, what do I care. I'm just happy to be off early."

I smile. "If you're happy, then I am too," I say.

Amalie leaves and I clean up after her, thinking I should have told her to do it herself, but also know why I didn't. She was finally so happy and we had a nice time together. I didn't want to ruin that.

"Learn to pick your battles carefully," I mumble to myself, quoting an article in my magazine about disciplining teenagers. I wash her dish and put away the bread. Then I walk to the playpen and pick up Josephine. I play with her on the floor till my husband comes home with Jacob. I put Josephine back in the playpen while I attend to my son and his needs. I kiss him and ask him about his day while finding a healthy snack for him in the kitchen.

"Did you have fun today in pre-school?" I ask.

He nods and eats the apple-bites I cut out for him. My husband takes a cup of coffee and loosens his tie.

"How was your day?" I ask.

He shrugs, while drinking his coffee. "Okay, I guess. Like most days. Trying to land the Boyesen account, but it's harder than expected."

"Well it will be yours, I'm certain," I say and cut up more apples for my son.

"I'm not so sure anymore," my husband says.

"What? How come?"

"Well I've been gone a lot lately so I'm afraid Martin will give it to Gert instead."

"He wouldn't!"

Christian shrugs again, then sips his coffee while slurping.

"Don't do that," I say.

He looks at me.

"Don't slurp the coffee, please."

Christian sighs then takes his cup and walks into the living room. I hear the TV turned on. I close my eyes and count to ten again. I debate within myself if I should go in there and tell him that the rule is *no TV in the afternoon*, but I restrain myself, repeating the sentence from my article: "Pick your battles carefully."

Jacob looks at me and smiles. I smile back. My husband returns to the kitchen and takes another cup of coffee and takes a bag of licorice out of the cupboard. I count to ten again, then speak anyway.

"Don't eat candy right before dinner," I say. "You know those salty things are bad for your blood-pressure and it'll ruin your appetite."

My husband opens the bag with a grin anyway, eats a handful, chewing them with his mouth wide open, smacking his lips.

I calm myself down.

"What's that?" my husband asks and points at my shirt. I look down and see a big red spot on my new white silk shirt.

"Blood," I say and try to wipe it off with a paper towel.

My husband laughs showing the black half-eaten licorice in his mouth. "Good one," he says. "Looks more like fruit-juice."

I take it off and throw it in the washer.

CHAPTER SIX

I **SERVE** *frikadeller,* Danish meatballs for dinner. They all look like they enjoy it. I have no appetite. I push a potato around with my fork. The silence gets on my nerves. I can hear my husband chew. The clock on the wall ticks too damn loud.

"Did you watch the news today?" Amalie asks.

Her father shakes his head. "No, what's new?"

"Someone was killed here in Karrebaeksminde."

My husband swallows loudly, then picks up his glass of wine I told him not to have on a weeknight, then gulps it down. "Really?"

"Yes a couple. They were stabbed in an alley in town. They think it was drug-related. They guy apparently owed a lot of money to some bad guys or something. But listen to this. They had a two-year-old with them when it happened, and apparently whoever did this dropped the child off at a day-care not far from there."

"Then they must have seen who it was?" Christian asked and drank again.

"No, apparently they didn't. They said he was left in a

stroller outside the door and then whoever brought him there rang the doorbell of the day-care and then ran off. Weird, huh?"

My husband nods slowly while chewing. "That *is* very strange."

"A killer with a conscience, that's nice," I say and smile.

"They say the kid was full of old bruises on his body once the doctors examined him."

I clench the fork in my hand till my knuckles turn white. Then I drop it on the plate. "Anyone in the mood for seconds?" I ask smiling.

I watch the news with my husband after all the children are in bed, but soon I get bored and go to bed too. I sleep for a few hours before Josephine wakes me up by crying. I go to her and sit with her for a couple of hours to calm her down. I feed her and rock her until she falls asleep in my arms. I stay with her all night, afraid to wake her up if I get up from the chair. I fall asleep with her in my arms. She wakes me up at dawn and I change her diaper before anyone else is up.

I change her clothes and bring her downstairs where I let her lie on a blanket while I prepare breakfast for the entire family and pack the kid's lunches. Jacob looks sad when he comes down.

"What's wrong buddy?" I ask while serving him his oatmeal.

"I don't want to go to pre-school today," he says.

"Why not? You know you have to go if you want to be a big boy and go to kindergarten next year like all the other kids."

"I just don't want to."

"What's wrong? Did something happen yesterday?"

Jacob is not eating. He just scoops the spoon around in the porridge.

"You can tell me Jacob. You can tell me anything."

"It's just Oliver. He is so mean."

"Oliver Bille?"

Jacob nods. I lean over and kiss his forehead. "What did he do, huh?"

"He hit me. On the playground. I didn't want to give him the car I was playing with, so he hit me."

"And what did you do?"

"I gave him the car and ran. Later when I was on the swing he came and said he wanted that too, then he pulled me off it so I scraped my knee." Jacob pulls up his pants to show me.

"How come you didn't show me this yesterday?" I ask startled.

"I thought you might be mad."

I caress his cheek gently, then lean over and kiss him again. "Oliver is the one being a bully. Why should I be mad at you, huh?"

Jacob shrugs and smiles when I tickle his stomach.

"Now eat," I say and push the bowl of oatmeal closer. "I'll drop you off today."

I gulp down my morning smoothie made from organic kiwis, honey, beet, ginger, and banana that according to the recipe is guaranteed to keep me satisfied until lunch and to keep me heart-healthy with its richness in polyphenols and vitamin C. Then I change Josephine again and put her in the car next to Jacob.

In the pre-school the staff greets me with gentle smiles and tells me it's so nice to finally see me again. I sign in Jacob and while I do I spot the boy Oliver saying goodbye to his father. After saying goodbye to Jacob, I decide to approach him. I run after him into the street carrying Josephine by the handle of her infant car seat where she has fallen asleep. He hurries to his car, a huge Mercedes. He is nicely dressed in an Armani suit when I poke his shoulder. He turns and looks at me annoyed.

"What?" he asks. "I'm kind of in a hurry to get to a meeting."

I smile, then put my baby down on the ground carefully, making sure she doesn't wake up. "I understand and acknowledge that completely," I say finding my very nice tone of voice. "But I need to talk to you about your son."

The father sighs, annoyed. Then he puts his arms up in front of him. "As I told you, I have a very busy day and this is not the time for this."

I grab his arm and hold on to it tight. "I'm sure you're a very, very important man, with many very, very important things to do, maybe even so important you hardly have time to talk to your son or even discipline him. But your son is a bully, and I'm beginning to see where he has got it from. Tell me, Mr. Bille, why are you in such a hurry? Is it because you're late for some big business meeting where you're planning on stepping on some innocent people on your way to the top? Or are you just late for your mistress who is waiting for you in the apartment you rented for your little love affair to take place in secrecy?"

Mr. Bille blushes and pulls his arm out of my grip. "What is this?" he asks. "Some kind of extortion? Who are you? How dare you to talk to me like this? Do you even know who I am?"

"No. I have a feeling you would love to tell me, but that's besides the point here."

Mr. Bille stares into my eyes, then blinks a couple of times, looking confused. "What is it you want?" He asks.

"What I WANT is for YOU to stop your SON from

bullying other children," I say and poke him in the chest while speaking.

"You're insane," he says, shaking his head.

I stomp my feet in the pavement. "See that's exactly what I am talking about. You people bully anyone you get in contact with and you get away with it. Uh, I HATE that."

"Listen to me, woman. I don't know who you are or how you know about my affair, but I tell you to leave it alone, leave me alone now, or I swear I'll call the police."

I close my eyes and count to ten. The kitchen knife in the pocket of my jacket feels sharp against my thigh.

Mr. Bille opens the door to his car while mumbling. "Crazy bitch, I don't know why I ..."

I open my eyes, then pull out the knife and stab him in the lower part of the stomach. The stab hits him midsentence. Startled he stares at me in fear. I'm still holding the handle of the knife in my hand. I pull it out, then lift it and stab Mr. Bille again, this time in the chest. Mr. Bille's eyes look up at me, and then roll back in his head. He tries to scream, but his mouth is full of blood. Besides no one would hear it in the noise from the construction-workers nearby who by the way see nothing. His hands are trying to grab the handle of the knife, but the stab wounds have sapped his strength. His body is shaking now and I step backwards while Mr. Bille's blood is running into the road. Some of it has sprayed onto my jacket, I notice, annoyed. Now I have to stop by the cleaners on my way home. Today of all days!

I stay and watch as Mr. Bille falls into the street with a deep groan. His face is pale and blood is running out from the corners of his mouth. He is still alive and tries to speak, probably even to scream, but nothing but a twisted groan springs out of his throat. His fight for survival is pathetic. Makes me want to stab him again, but I decide he's not worth the effort. Will probably just bleed to death within the next five-six minutes. I lean over and pull out the knife from his chest. A river of blood flushes out from the wound. I wipe the knife in his Armani jacket, then put it in my purse. I pick up Josephine and start to walk back to my car.

There was another grammatical error in Rebekka Franck's article in today's paper about yesterday's killings in an alley downtown. Tonight I'll serve spaghetti and meat sauce.

———————

CHAPTER SEVEN

"THE POLICE came to the school today," Amalie says during dinner.

I hardly blink as I speak. "Really? What did they want?" I roll the spaghetti neatly onto my spoon before I put it in my mouth. I'm careful to not eat too much of this food that is so rich in carbs. Tonight I'll give Christian that blowjob, I think while chewing.

"They were looking for Mr. Berendsen," Amalie says. "He's been missing for two days now."

"Well that's because I killed him," I say, rolling yet another perfectly shaped roll of spaghetti onto my spoon.

My daughter rolls her eyes at me. "Ha ha. Very funny, Mom. No, seriously they are really worried that something happened to him. They say they found his finger in the house or something."

"His finger?" Christian asks.

"Yeah, apparently the dog was chewing on it. They didn't find the rest of him though. But rumors say that his blood was smeared all over the walls of the kitchen."

"So they think he was killed?" Christian asks.

I grab the bowl of salad and pull it closer. I pour a big pile onto my plate.

"I guess so," Amalie says. "It's kind of creepy."

"Oh, nonsense," I say. "People are killed every day on this planet. Makes more room for the rest of us, am I right?"

Amalie chuckles. "You're funny, Mom."

"He was a bastard anyway," I say and eat my salad. It crunches in my head, sounding like when I chopped through Mr. Berendsen's bones with the axe I found in his garage. "So how do you like the meat?"

"It's delicious," Christian says. "It has like an extra flavor, I can't really detect. What is it?"

"The secret's in the sauce," I say with a grin quoting one of my favorite movies Fried Green tomatoes.

"That's so gross, Mom," Amalie says knowing where the quote comes from since I have forced her to watch it with me a million times.

Then we both laugh. Christian feels left out since he has never seen the movie. Jacob is eating without listening to the conversation as usual, smearing meat sauce all over his face and into his hair. I smile and hand him a napkin thinking it looks like the blood on Mr. Berendsen's walls, blood and chunks of meat.

I go to bed early after watching the news about a man being stabbed to death in the middle of the street. My husband nods off after three minutes and I sneak upstairs after kissing him gently on the cheek.

As always Josephine keeps me up most of the night. I sit with her in the rocking chair, giving her my breast while watching the moon outside the window in the nursery. I'm tired but still feel energized. I fall asleep in the rocking chair with Josephine in my arms and don't wake up until Christian comes in. He kneels next to me, then kisses me on the cheek.

"Sleep in here again tonight?" he asks.

I nod, careful not to wake up Josephine. Christian's eyes are sad when he looks at me. He strokes my hair, then kisses me again.

"You'll be late for work," I say.

He nods without a word, then leaves to get himself ready. I put Josephine in her crib, then turn on the baby-alarm before I wake up Amalie. Jacob is already up and playing with his cars in his room. I find his clothes and help him get dressed. I drink a simple organic orange, apple, kiwi-smoothie, then help everyone get out the door. As the house goes quiet I pick up the paper and read Rebekka Franck's latest article about the man getting killed in the parking lot downtown yesterday. No witnesses have so far come forward which worries the police since the murder was committed in broad daylight and someone must have at least seen something. I find a typo in the second paragraph and call them up to let them know. The lady tells me she'll let them know, as usual. I hang up, get myself ready to go and apply for a passport for Josephine for our trip to France this summer.

Tonight I'll be making my famous oven-dish.

CHAPTER EIGHT

I **PICK** a number at the Citizen's Department and sit down. Josephine is sleeping in the carriage that I place in the corner. I'm number five hundred thirty-eight. The next in line is number eighteen. The place is packed with people. Kids are playing, some are running around, others are crying. It's only nine in the morning but people look tired already. Their long faces stare at the screen hanging from the ceiling where the numbers are displayed. *Now serving number nineteen* someone says over the loudspeaker. I'm rocking the carriage to make sure Josephine won't wake up from all the noise. I prepare myself to sit here a long time and hope Josephine will sleep through it all. I find a magazine and flip through it. I read about the crown-prince and the princess and their four kids. They have been to some gala last week and both look wonderful, he in his uniform and she in her amazing dress. Well, it's easy to look great when you have that many people working for you making sure you do and taking care of your kids, I think to myself and put down the magazine. I find one of my favorite magazines called *Mama* and even if it's an issue I've already read I still find an article I can't remember having read before. *Are children allowed to cry themselves to sleep?* is the title of the article. It's the story of a family and how they all sleep together to make the children feel more comfortable at night. I scoff while reading it, since I think it's just an excuse for not wanting to discipline children properly. Are they supposed to sleep together when they're a teenager still? I wonder. Irritated with people's idiotic ideas I throw the magazine down on the table. I glance at the big screen, still only at number twenty-four. I check on Josephine, she's still sleeping. I pull off the cover to the carriage to make sure she's not too hot. She looks so peaceful while she's sleeping.

An hour and a half later it's finally my turn. My number is shown at the screen and someone calls for five hundred thirty-eight to please go to desk five. I grab the carriage and push it towards the window. I park it next to me and sit down. A woman is sitting on the other side of the glass. She looks like she hates me, but I'm thinking she probably just hates her job.

"Yes?" she asks.

"I'm here to apply for a passport for my baby," I say.

"Do you have the papers?" she asks.

I hand them to her through the opening in the glass. "I think it should be all there. We're going to France this summer, that's why I need a passport for her."

"Hmmm," the lady answers while going through the papers. She puts on her glasses, taps on her computer then looks at the screen. She turns and looks at me above her glasses. "Where is the baby now?" she asks.

"She's sleeping."

"I can't make a passport for a sleeping child," she says.

"I beg your pardon?"

The woman sighs. A sign in her window tells me her name is Susse Egholm. "I can't make a passport to a child I haven't seen. I need to see her face to make sure she is the child on the picture that was taken."

"But she's sleeping. Listen she's only three months old, I promise you it's her in the picture."

"I'm sorry," she says without any feeling to the words. "I can't finish your application before I have seen the child."

"What if you came out here and look at her face?"

"I need to see her eyes to be sure it's really her," she says. "Those are the rules."

I close my eyes and count to ten to calm myself down. "Listen ... Susse ... you seem like a nice person, can't you just make an exception. My baby has been awake all night and she really needs her sleep."

Susse Egholm shrugs. "I'm sorry ... rules are rules."

I clench my fist where she can't see it. I calm myself down again. I try once again to reason with her. "Do you have children?"

Susse Egholm shakes her head. "I don't see what that has to do with it," she says. "But no. I haven't had the honor. I hear it's a real hoot."

"So you don't know what it is like to stay up night after night with your baby trying desperately to get her to sleep, you don't know what it is like to finally be able to have her fall asleep while you're so exhausted you can barely stand up straight."

Susse shakes her head. "Listen, lady. If you don't want to wake the baby up, you can come back later and show her to me once she's awake. But you'll have to get back in the line."

"And wait another hour and a half?"

"Probably, yes."

I close my eyes and clench my fist till my nails hurt the palm of my hand.

"Or you could wake up the baby right now and get it over with."

I give Susse Egholm the finger, then run out of the center pushing Josephine in the carriage in front of me.

CHAPTER NINE

I USE the back entrance. It's afternoon when I walk into the Department and find Susse Egholm sitting behind a desk in her office. She's eating a piece of chocolate cake with her fingers while typing on the computer.

I walk in and park Josephine by the door, then I close it and make sure it is locked behind me. Josephine has fallen asleep again after being awake during my lunch. Susse Egholm lifts her head and looks at me as I approach her desk.

"You're not allowed to be in here," she says.

"And yet here I am," I say.

"Besides I'm not handling customers from here. I'm on my way home. Is the baby awake yet?" she asks.

"She was earlier, but the center was closed for lunch-break from noon till two and lucky me, it didn't open till she had fallen asleep again."

Susse Egholm swallows another bite of her chocolate cake. She wipes her fingers in her napkin. Crumbs fall onto the carpet. She has a small piece stuck between two of her teeth as she speaks. "Listen, lady. You have to get back and pick a number if you want to have this done, and this time wake the baby up, for crying out loud. Only for a few seconds and then she can go right back to sleep again."

"You don't know much about babies, do you?" I ask. "Then you'd know that they don't go back to sleep again once you wake them up like that. It's written in all the magazines, you DON'T WAKE UP A BABY!"

Startled Susse Egholm pulls her chair backwards and drops half of the cake onto the floor. "Get out," she says. "Get out of here before I call for security."

Her hand is on the phone. I pick up the stapler and staple one into her hand. "What are you doing, crazy bitch?" she yells.

I turn the stapler and give her a series of blows to the head with the heavy side of it. She tries to scream, but I pick up my Mace from my purse and spray it into her mouth to shut her up. I spray some in her eyes and nostrils as well. She is still making too much noise, though, so I find her jacket and place it over her head to drown out the gurgling screams. I keep shooting staples into her hands and face until it's empty. Then I pick up the keyboard and start hammering it over her head till she lies still. I remove the jacket and find a razor sharp paperknife. I stick it up her nose and cut her nostrils open. She wakes up momentarily, screaming, but I stuff her mouth with post-its and tape and yank it into her throat using a pencil. She tries to throw up, but I hold her head backwards till she chokes in her own vomit. Her body shakes for a little while, then gives in.

I decide to forget about my diet for a few minutes and eat the rest of her chocolate cake on my way out.

When driving home I pass several police cars driving in the opposite direction. I wonder if Christian has landed that Boyesen account yet as I swing the car into the driveway and park it in the garage. Josephine is awake the rest of the afternoon and I play with her while my dish simmers in the oven.

Christian comes home looking tired but Jacob tells me he had a wonderful day. Amalie is happier than ever, since she has a new math-teacher now, she tells me, and she is nice and will let her pass the class if she aces the next test which I make her promise that she will.

"I'll go study for it right away," she says and runs to her room.

I put Josephine in the playpen, while I allow Jacob to watch a cartoon for once and go into the kitchen to talk to my husband. He's upset and has taken a beer from the refrigerator. He is going through the drawers.

"That bad, huh?" I ask.

"Hmm," he answers.

I walk past him, pull out another drawer and find a package of cigarettes that I hand him. He smiles and takes them. I follow him to the terrace where he lights it up. He hands it to me. I shrug.

"Why not?" I ask and take it. "We all have to die somehow, right?" The taste reminds me of being in my twenties and meeting Christian at a party at a friend's house. Back when everybody smoked. I laugh at the memory. Christian smiles. Then he grows serious.

"I'm losing the account," he says.

I blow out smoke, then give the cigarette back to him. "To Gert?"

Christian nods. "Martin told me today that he was sorry, but Gert has been doing a great job lately and I have hardly been there."

"That's bullshit and he knows it," I say. "You work as hard as anyone."

Christian shrugs and looks down. "It has been a little

hard lately. To focus, I mean. Plus I have been away too much. I've had to leave early and come in late some days, in order to help you out."

"Yeah, but still ..."

"It's all that it takes," he says. "Even if they know our situation, with the baby and all ... well they can't take any special consideration, not when it comes to something this important. That's just the way it is."

I close my eyes and try to sing a calming song inside of my head. The only one I can come to think of is *Rock-a-bye baby*, I try it anyway, and it doesn't help. I'm still furious.

"I'm going to kill Gert," I say. "Him and his stupid *I don't look old because I have Botox three times a month* -wife."

Christian laughs while blowing smoke out of his mouth. "I guess I feel the same way every once in a while."

CHAPTER TEN

I'M ALREADY awake when Josephine cries at two o'clock in the morning. I haven't closed an eye all night. I can't stop thinking about that awful couple Gert and his even worse wife Marianne.

When I hear Josephine I go to her and feed her while staring at the dirt in the corner of the room. A small ball of hair and dirt that I hadn't noticed earlier when I cleaned the house. I can see it even though I have only lit a small lamp in the corner of the room. In the dirt I keep seeing Marianne's Botoxed face. She's grinning at me. As soon as Josephine is done eating I make my decision. I change her diaper, then bring her with me in the carriage where she falls asleep while I walk in the dark night pushing her in front of me, gently rocking her till she makes no noise anymore.

I wake them up by throwing apples in their faces. I brought the bag from home. They're organic, naturally. Gert wakes up when the first red apple hits his forehead.

"What the hell?" he says and tries to cover his face when another apple hits his cheek.

Then his wife Marianne opens her eyes as well. I throw an apple at her and hit her on the mouth. It hurts, I can tell by her reaction. Gert reaches for the night lamp and lights it. They see me between apples flying. I'm smiling while throwing.

"Lisa?" Marianne says. I can tell by the tone of her voice that she is surprised, confused even.

"What the hell are you doing?" Gert yells and sits up in the bed while still covering his head with his arm.

"Throwing apples," I say while another hits him in the forehead and knocks him backwards. I have always had a good arm. Used to play handball and could throw the hardest on the team. I'm wondering if any of my kids can throw as well as I used to, then wonder if they could make it farther than I ever did. Maybe go on the national team?

"Stop throwing apples at us!" Marianne yells.

One hits her face and breaks. Juice runs across her cheek while pieces of apple splatter in her face.

"Ouch! Goddammit Lisa! That really hurt."

I laugh a madman's laughter. I can't help it. Gert is out of bed now and storms towards me. I smile and tilt my head as he tries to grab my arms. I pull out my knife and stab him in the stomach. His eyes grow wide in surprise as he tries to touch the handle of the knife. Marianne starts screaming. I throw another apple in her face, but she keeps screaming and tries to get out of the bed. While Gert is bending forward and moaning I walk to Marianne with an apple in my hand. She screams and tries to get away from me. I grab her hair and pull her towards me. Then I stuff the apple into her mouth to shut her up. Her jaw sounds like it breaks as I push it in. She tries to scream but only a muffled sound comes out of her, then she tries to close her mouth, but can't, she even tries to chew and destroy the apple, but it's impossible. It's too big and I'm holding her hands so she can't pull it out either. I can tell she's struggling to breathe through her nose, so I hold it a few seconds just for fun. Then I tie up her hands with some of my husband's duct tape that he uses to fix anything even if I think it looks terrible. I tie up her legs as well. I hope Josephine is still sleeping in the baby carriage that I placed in the living room when I walked in the kitchen door to the house that they carelessly had left unlocked. I hope the noise hasn't woken her up. It's three a.m. and I'm thinking of making homemade sausages for dinner tonight. As I pull Marianne by the hair out of the bedroom and down the stairs making her body bump all of the steps on her way down, I'm thinking that I'll give Jacob some of my homemade spelt rolls in his lunch box today. Gotta make sure he eats healthy and gets healthy habits from a young age, I repeat from an article I read earlier in the day. Or was it yesterday? I don't know anymore.

Marianne is crying when I place her on the kitchen floor. I don't have time to feel bad for her. I find a stack of old newspapers that I spread out across the floor to cover the nice, clean tiles. Then I go upstairs and find Gert lying on the floor. He is still moaning. He has tried to move towards the phone by the bed but not gotten very far. I shake my head, then take the lamp and slam it into the back of his head knocking him unconscious. I make a trail of blood across the nice beige carpet as I drag him towards the stairs and lift him with much difficulty over the railing and let him fall downstairs, hitting a table and knocking down the family pictures that were neatly placed on top of it. Blood is smeared all over the pictures of their grown daughter standing with her high school diploma. I don't have time to clean it up. I pull Gert's hand and drag him into the kitchen and place him on the newspapers. Marianne lets out a whimper when she sees him. She is trying to kick and scream, but as soon as I start the chainsaw, I can't hear her anymore.

CHAPTER ELEVEN

I'M STILL working the meat grinder when Christian comes into the kitchen the next morning. He looks tired, I think.

"There is coffee in the pot," I say.

He looks around in the kitchen. Ground meat is lying in huge stacks. "Have you been up all night cooking or something?" he asks.

I smile and nod. "Thought I'd make homemade sausages for tonight."

"For an entire army?" he asks.

"Well I was gonna freeze some for another day."

Christian shakes his head and rubs his hair. "I don't think we have enough room in the freezer for all this." He watches as the red meat comes out of the small holes in the end of the grinder and falls into a big dish I have placed underneath.

"Well I bought a new freezer yesterday," I say and put more meat in the top, then work the handle. "Or was it last week? I don't remember anymore. I had them place it in the basement."

"Where did you get all this meat from?" he asks and looks at the big black bag next to me.

"Oh, that. That's just someone I killed last night."

Christian yawns and then chuckles. He walks over to the pot and pours himself a cup. Then he shakes his head slowly. "No seriously, did you get it from the butcher again, cause it looks like there is a lot of meat there, and it must have been expensive. We won't have much money now that I've lost the account."

I smile and tilt my head. I have a tic in my left eye that won't seem to go away. I ignore it. "I promise it wasn't expensive."

Christian walks to the counter and looks at the ground meat. "Looks good though," he says and sips his coffee. "Can't wait."

"I know you love those sausages I make."

Christian drinks from his coffee again. "Will you make them Italian Hot sausages the way I like them best?"

"I'll make sure some of them are hot just for you."

Christian leans over and kisses my cheek. I place a piece of meat in the grinder and turn the handle.

"I better get dressed and get ready for work," Christian sighs. "Today Martin is gonna choose who gets the Boyesen account. I've dreaded this for days, but there's no way to avoid it. Guess I just have to take it like a man, right?"

"I'm certain you'll enjoy your day."

Christian smiles at me. "It's good to have you back. Seems like you've been more yourself lately."

"I didn't know I've been gone," I say.

"You know what I mean," he says and kisses me again. "I'm glad you keep yourself busy, just make sure you get some sleep today, promise me that?"

"I'll try."

Later in the day I go to the butcher and buy all of his hog casings to stuff with the meat. I tell him I'll be back tomorrow for more since I have many sausages to do. At home I stuff as many as I have with help from my sausage stuffer that I got for Christmas. Then I make some of them by using blanched savoy cabbage leaves as a wrapper. I put those aside for myself thinking they're healthier and that I will never get my husband to eat them, or the children for that matter. The rest of the meat I put in the new freezer along with the hundreds of sausages I've made. I have to rearrange a little to make room for all the meat, so I take out Mr. Berendsen's head and let him sit on the table next to me while I make room for the rest. Mr. Berendsen looks at me slightly disappointed, I think when I put him back in with the rest of his body, or what is left of it.

Amalie is happy when she comes home later in the day and we drink herbal tea together in the kitchen while she tells me about her day. I enjoy being with her and love seeing her this happy again.

"It's still a mystery what happened to Mr. Berendsen," she says. "Not that I mind, but the police came again today to ask questions. It kind of scared me."

"They're just doing their job," I answer while the tic in my right eye grows worse. Wait wasn't it in the left eye earlier? I shake my head and drink my tea. I wonder if I have eaten at all today. I can't seem to remember. Have I even read the paper? I can't recall reading Rebekka Franck's latest article. Maybe I already did. Yes, that's it. I already read it. There was a misspelling in the fourth paragraph. Or was it in the third? I don't know. Maybe it doesn't matter. Amalie is still talking. I try and listen in, but so much information is running through my head. Amalie tells me she loves her new math teacher and that she doesn't mind if Mr. Berendsen is gone, but at the same time, she feels bad if anything bad happened to him. I nod and smile, while thinking that I have nothing to serve along with the sausages. You can't just eat sausages alone. I need to go buy potatoes or maybe pasta? Too many carbs. I'll make a salad, I decide.

"Am I a bad person for thinking this way?" my daughter asks. "In my defense, Mr. Berendsen was really mean to many of the students. I don't think you'll see anyone being sad that he's gone."

"We all have to die at some point, honey," I say and pat the top of her hand. "Some people just deserve to die earlier."

Amalie looks at me strangely. "What do you mean, Mom? You think he was killed?"

"Well there was blood in his house, right?"

"Yeah, but they haven't found his body or anything. Just his finger." Amalie shivers slightly by saying it. I feel nothing. I'm thinking about Josephine. I don't seem to recall where I put her. Is she sleeping? Yes that has to be it, I think. I get up from the chair and walk to the living room. The playpen is empty. So she must be in her bed, I think and walk upstairs. My daughter follows me to the stairs.

"Are you alright, Mom?" she asks.

"I'm fine honey," I say without looking at her.

I walk into the nursery but find the bed empty. A panic starts to spread. Has something happened to her? Did I forget her somewhere? At the butcher's? At the grocery store? I feel the room spinning around me and I can't seem to make my mind stand still. If only I could remember, if only I could get a picture of where I had her last. I run down the stairs feeling panic rising. Amalie looks at me with concern.

"Do you want me to call Dad?" she asks.

"No, no. You mustn't do that," I say. I grab her shoulders and shake her heavily. "Promise me you won't call your dad!"

"Okay. Okay," she says.

I let go of her and storm out the door. The baby carriage is gone! It is not in my front yard where I always put it. Someone has taken my baby carriage and my baby! In the street I spot my neighbor. A woman in her thirties who hasn't been able to have a child. Suddenly it strikes me. *She has taken mine!* I always had a feeling about her, I think as I run towards her. She is walking towards my house and she is ... yes she is pushing my baby carriage in front of her! I run towards her feeling the anger rise. She is smiling and waving.

"Hi there, neighbor," she yells and waves.

I approach her while my hands are shaking heavily. I imagine killing her with my bare hands, strangling her while looking into her eyes and letting her know that nobody, nobody takes my baby.

"I found this in my front yard," she says and points at the blue carriage. "Is it yours?"

I reach out and push her away from the carriage. Then I slam my fist into her face forcing her to stumble backwards with a shriek.

I grab the carriage by the handle and start to push it towards my house. Josephine is awake and now she is looking at me. I smile at her while promising her that no one is ever going to take her from me again. As I pick her up and walk inside I'm thinking I'll make potato salad as a side dish.

CHAPTER TWELVE

I **HAVE** barely put Josephine down in the playpen before my husband storms through the front door. I look at him startled.

"What are you doing home this early?" I ask.

"Are you okay?" he asks.

I shake my head. "Am *I* okay? What do you mean by that?"

"Amalie called and told me you were freaking out."

"She did what? I told her not to call you. Well I'm fine. As you can see everything is just fine. I've just been stressed out a little lately. You know not enough sleep and all."

Christian nods and smiles. "I'm relieved that everything is well," he says. "I actually have great news ..."

"Really?" I ask. Josephine is fussing and I rub her belly gently.

"Yes. I got the account!"

I smile from ear to ear. "You got it?"

He nods and I jump up and hug him. "I'm so happy for you my love."

"I can hardly believe it myself," he says and sets down his

briefcase. "When the meeting started today Gert never showed up. Can you believe that? Martin was so angry he immediately signed the account over to me."

"That is wonderful news," I say and kiss Christian on the lips.

We should celebrate," Christian says.

"Let's have some sausages!" I exclaim.

Christian shakes his head. "No. I mean let's go out. Just the two of us. We'll get a nanny."

I look at Josephine in the playpen, then shake my head. "I don't ..." Then I pause. I can hardly explain to my husband how I almost lost her today and how I am determined to never let her out of my sight again. Trusting my baby with a stranger isn't something I feel ready for just yet.

"Come on," he says. "Let's go out for once. It's been far too long."

I look into his eyes. I wonder if I should give him the blowjob now and maybe that'll make him forget about going out? I'm not sure it's enough.

"Where will you get a nanny with this short notice?" I ask.

"One of the new guys at the office, Karl, gave me the number of his nanny, when I told him I was planning on taking you out to celebrate tonight. I can call her right now and see if she's available."

"I don't know, Christian. I'm worried about this. She doesn't even know the kids."

Christian picks up the phone and dials a number. "We're doing this," he says. "We need to live a little."

I look down at Josephine while Christian walks into the kitchen with the phone. I hear him talk to someone. Josephine is cooing happily. My belly rub helped her. I'm sweating anxiously. How am I supposed to leave her home all alone?

My husband returns looking happy. I feel a panic rise inside of me.

"Done," he says with a huge grin. "She'll be here at five thirty and you can introduce her to the kids and show her around before we leave. Okay?"

I force a smile while feeling the desperation plant small chills on my back. What do we even know about this girl? I think. She could be a mass-murderer, she could be a psychopath, part of a pedophile ring that steals small children and sends them to Eastern Europe to raise them on those farms, I saw on TV, where they use them for all kinds of atrocities. Maybe she herself is a pedophile, maybe she'll hurt my little daughter somehow, and exploiting the fact that she cannot tell on her afterwards?

While my husband whistles and goes into the kitchen to grab himself a beer from the refrigerator I take Josephine into my arms and kiss her cheeks till she starts fussing again. I bring her with me into the kitchen clinging on to her tight.

"What about all the sausages then?" I ask.

CHAPTER THIRTEEN

THE NANNY turns out to be a sixteen-year-old girl and at first sight she doesn't seem like she could hurt a fly, let alone a child. She tells me she is a student at the local high school, and her parents are out of town this week so it's okay if it gets late even if it is a school night. Then she gives me a list of references to people she has been a nanny for the last couple of years. She knows CPR and is a trained lifeguard in case any of the children should come near water which I tell her they never will and that I will make sure to kill her if they do. She laughs thinking I'm joking and I finally agree to leave the lives of my loved ones in her hands. Josephine is asleep when we leave and I hope she will stay like that until we come back. Just to make sure that the nanny, Lucille is prepared I show her where the changing table is and leave a bottle of pumped out breast milk in the refrigerator. She seems a little confused at first and I am almost having second thoughts, but my husband calls for me from downstairs and I decide to give him the evening he so dreams off. Maybe I will even give him that blow-job when we come home, I think as I say goodbye to Lucille and let my husband drag me out of the house to the taxi waiting on the street outside. As the door closes behind me I feel a shiver of anxiety and I'm almost about to turn around but Christian's grip on my hand is tight and determined and a few seconds later I find myself in the backseat of the taxi looking back at the house where I have left my babies in the hands of a high school mass-murderer.

The dinner is good even though I hardly touch it. I'm thinking about Lucille alone with the children and regret that I forgot to tell her about the sausages in the refrigerator that she could give the kids for dinner.

"You're hardly eating," Christian says and empties his third glass of wine. "You haven't been eating much lately at all," he says.

"I forgot to tell them about the sausages," I say.

"Well forget about the sausages. We'll eat them tomorrow. And the day after that. Lord knows there's enough for a long time, right?"

"But I was really looking forward to having sausages tonight," I say. "I spent all night preparing them, chopping the meat off the bones."

Christian smiles and grabs my hand. "It's good to be alone like this," he says. "It's been way too long since we have been just the two of us. I've really missed it. I've missed you."

I look up from my plate and look into his eyes. He's smiling, dazed by the wine. "I really love you Lisa," he says.

His eyes are warm, gentle and the light from the candle is reflected in them. I can't stop thinking what his eyeballs would look like if I poked my fork into them. I smile back. He takes my hand and kisses the top of it. I imagine chopping his off by the wrist.

"Maybe you want a blow-job later?" I ask and finally eat

some of my scallops. They're way too salty for my taste. "When we get home?"

Christian almost chokes on his wine. He spits some of it out on the white tablecloth. It looks like blood sprayed on a white wall. Christian grins and holds a hand to his mouth. "You're really something," he says.

"I think the sausages needed more nutmeg," I say.

Christian shakes his head and laughs, then the waiter pours him another glass of wine. We toast and drink some more. The wine seems to calm down my mind, but it leaves me confused and strangely out of control. I feel like the room is spinning and hold onto the table to not fall down.

"Are you alright?" Christian asks.

"I'm perfect," I say and let go of the table. I'm getting used to the spinning now and quite enjoying it. It's fun; I think and try to catch things as they fly around me at great speed. Christian is smiling and toasting again. The wine is warm and makes me fuzzy, my sight gets blurry and soon everything goes black.

I wake up feeling thirsty. I walk down the stairs and get a glass out of the cupboard. I pour water into it and drink while watching the full moon outside my kitchen window. I wonder how we got home. I don't seem to remember anything. My head begins to hurt. I open my eyes widely.

"Josephine," I say out loud and throw the glass in the sink and run upstairs. I storm into the nursery. I breathe a sigh of relief. Josephine is still sleeping. I look at her in the darkness and smile, then look at the Winnie The Pooh clock on the wall. It's almost two o'clock. About the time she normally wakes up. There is no need to go to bed again, I tell myself and sit in the rocking chair and wait for her to wake up. Again I wonder about the dinner and how we got home. Did we take a taxi? I simply don't remember. I shake my head feeling like a young girl again after a night in town with the girls, not remembering what I have done the next day. Then I remember something. I think I did give Christian that blow-job last night. I clearly remember having it in my mouth. Or maybe it was a sausage. I have no way of knowing.

Josephine makes a sound and I go to look at her. She is tossing and turning in her sleep. That's when I realize something is wrong. Something is very wrong. My baby is lying on her stomach! And she has a blanket over her body. Terrified by this I pick her up, while my heart is beating fast. I hold her close to me, then breathe relieved once again. I listen to her breaths for a long time, relieved that I noticed this fatal mistake that the nanny had made in time. I can hardly think the thought to an end. *The nanny almost killed my baby!*

CHAPTER FOURTEEN

I **CAN'T** stop thinking about it. I feed Josephine for at least an hour. I can tell she missed me by the way she clings to my breast and won't let go even if I can tell she is full. Every time I try and pull her away because she's asleep, she wakes up and starts fussing. I let her stay close to me for another half an hour, then put her in the baby carriage and go for a walk in the hope that it will make her fall back to sleep.

I find myself outside a house. I have a note that I'm clenching in my fist. It's the nanny's address that she gave to me before I left her alone with my children earlier in the evening. I'm sweating even if it is a cold night. Josephine is finally asleep again in the carriage. I'm wearing nothing but a light nightgown. The wind goes right through it, but I'm still not cold.

The house is dark and the wind is pulling on the big birch in the front yard. Its thin crooked branches are swaying lightly making it look like arms reaching out to grab me.

I kick down the back door to the house, not caring what kind of noise I'm making. Then I storm inside pushing the carriage in front of me.

I find the girl in one of the rooms in the back of the house. I realize I don't know if she's an only child or if there could be someone else in the house. I decide I don't care and push the carriage through the door to her room. She wakes up immediately and starts to scream. I slam my baby's toxin-free organic glass bottle into her face. She screams in pain. I move quickly while she is still startled by the sudden attack. I take a couple of diapers out of the bag and stuff them into her throat to drown out the noise. Finally only muffled sounds are coming from her. She's fighting me but I'm too strong, plus she is skinny and I am able to hold her down with the extra weight I gained during my last pregnancy. I tape her arms together with duct tape and her legs as well. She's still fighting, so I hit her with the bottle again, while thinking how amazingly sustainable it is. Her eyes roll back in her head and she is fighting to stay conscious. I hit her again. This time it leaves a big, bloody wound. I get some on my night-gown and sigh annoyed.

"Now I have to wash this," I mumble.

Then I swing the bottle again and knock her out. I glance over at Josephine in the carriage. Luckily she didn't wake from all the noise and turmoil. I look at the nanny and shake my head heavily. She is coming back now slowly. I watch her as she opens her eyes and tries to figure out if it was all a dream. Then she realizes it isn't and stares at me with wide-open eyes. I smile and wave at her. New muffled sounds comes from behind the diapers. I have put duct tape across her mouth to force them to stay in. She's choking on them, I can tell. Gagging and trying hard not to throw up. I look at her in contempt.

"To think I let you alone with my children. So irresponsible," I say. I get agitated just by thinking about what she has done. I am sweating a lot now and try to wipe the drops of sweat off my upper lip with my hand, but it's not enough. I use a blouse I find on the floor. "Messy too, huh?" I say to the girl who has stopped trying to scream and is now staring at me in distrust. "Hasn't your mother taught you anything?"

I wipe off my face in the blouse. The white in it turns red and I realize I have her blood all over my face. I wipe my entire face with it, then fold it neatly together and put it into my bag. I'm not so stupid I'm going to leave evidence like that around after me. I look at the girl. Her eyes are fearful. I tilt my head and smile.

"You know I have to hurt you now, don't you?"

She utters a muffled sound that I think is a gasp, then nods her head slowly. Her eyes are filled with tears. I don't feel pity for her. After all she almost killed my child. Now she has to pay.

"I mean I can't let a thing like that go unpunished. You almost killed my BABY," I say and point at the carriage.

She looks like she doesn't understand. I sigh and try to explain.

"Don't you know how to put down a baby?" I ask.

She stares at me like she doesn't know what to do. Then she nods.

"Well then you should know, that babies MUST NOT SLEEP ON THEIR STOMACHS!"

As I yell the words I take out the kitchen knife and stab it into her leg. It makes a crunching sound. She moans something. Then I pull it out again. She is crying hard now.

"Don't you know anything?" I say. "If you put them down on their stomach they will SUFFOCATE." I sigh again, then stab her in the other leg. She groans in pain.

"I mean it's in all the books, for crying out loud. You can read about it in every magazine there is about babies. SIDS is the most common killer of little babies and they are almost always found lying on their stomachs when they are dead, suffocated. And on top of it, you put her blanket in with her?" I pull out the knife and stab her again, in the thigh this time.

"A blanket she can get over her head and it can block her breathing! She is so small she can't remove it herself. Don't you KNOW that?" I raise the knife again and stab her in the stomach. "No, blankets," I say when I pull it out and stab her in the chest. "And always ... Always put the baby on its back!"

On the last word I stab her once again in the chest and warm blood spurts out on my face and all over my night-gown. I keep stabbing her till she hardly moves anymore. Then I try to flay her, to cut off her skin while she is still - barely - alive. But it's more difficult than it sounds and I have to give it up half way. The room is a mess when the girl finally takes her final breath. Blood is on all the walls, pieces of her skin is spread on the bed. I don't know what to do with it all and certainly have no more room in my freezer, nor any desire to make more sausages.

I decide to burn the house down. I leave the gas-stove open, then light a match and throw it in through the door. The pressure wave from the blast pushes me and the baby-carriage in the back as we walk down the street. I never turn to look back at the explosive fire.

CHAPTER FIFTEEN

R EBEKKA FRANCK has an article in the paper about last night's explosion in the nice neighborhood just north of us. I shake my head while drinking a cherry, cabbage and cinnamon smoothie. There is a grammatical error in the last paragraph. I tell Christian and show him, he says he can't see it. I think he just doesn't care. I tell the kids to eat their breakfast. Christian is whistling happily. I am thinking I must have given him that blow-job after all. I smile and look at my family. Amalie is happy and for once on time for school. Jacob tells me he can't wait to get to pre-school and Christian is excited about starting a new day at the office and begin taking care of the Boyesen account.

"Maybe we should go to The Maldives this fall," he says. "With the extra money I'm making now there should be a little extra for more vacation."

"That sounds wonderful, darling," I say and kiss him when he leans over to say goodbye.

Everything is perfect, I think as I watch my family take off with smiling faces. Everything but ... I think as the house goes quiet. My eyes keep focusing on the article on the table.

"Everything but this," I say out loud and tap my finger on the error in the article. It is bothering me that she keeps making these mistakes and even more that no one else at the paper seems to care enough to correct her or at least catch the mistakes before the article is printed. The more I think about it, the worse I feel inside. I try to calm myself down, then I pick up the phone and call the paper. I let them know that there is another mistake today and that I think they should do something about all those errors soon. "It's a disgrace to the reader," I say in contempt. I hang up without saying goodbye. Josephine is awake and I go to her in the playpen. I lean over and receive one of her smiles. I tickle her stomach gently.

"We're not going to let people just disrespect us, will we? No we're not. No, we are not," I say and tap her stomach with my fingers causing her to smile again.

"People should know when they make a mistake. It should be corrected," I continue. "Where will it leave us if no body corrected anybody anymore? Everybody would just be imperfect and full of mistakes, yes they would. Yes they would. And we can't have that, now can we? No we can't."

Josephine makes a frowning face and I laugh. "Seems like we agree on the matter," I say.

I leave Josephine to play with her owl made from organic cotton and non-toxic materials. I walk into the kitchen and empty my smoothie while obsessing about the article. It is still lying on the table in front of me and I feel like it's looking back at me, almost mocking me. I try to leave it alone and focus on cleaning up after breakfast. I wonder what to prepare for dinner. I decide on making a Swedish dish with sausages, paprika and potatoes. I wash the dishes but feel like the article is calling me from the table. I breathe heavily and try to stay calm. The sentence carrying the error is in my head, it's repeated over and over again. I wipe the plates clean and put them back in the cupboard. Then I pull everything out of the cupboard again and wipe the shelves clean before I put all the plates back again and place them straight in a line. I turn all the cups next to them to face the same way. Then I move on to the next cupboard where I pull out all of the cans and boxes. I put them back, sorting them alphabetically and making all the labels face outwards. I close the cupboard, then move on to the counter. I wipe it down with a disinfecting cloth and arrange everything so it looks neat. I'm sweating again and can't seem to stop. I find a towel and wipe it off, but more keep coming. I smell bad, I realize. So I walk upstairs and take a shower to wash it off. I scrub my body with a sponge, till stripes of blood run down my leg. Then I stop. I walk downstairs after drying my hair. My skin is hurting from all the scrubbing and the black pants I'm wearing rub against the abrasions. I make myself a decaf skinny latte and stare at the pile of newspaper clippings in the corner. There is a whole stack that I have placed on the counter as neatly as possible with a rubber band holding them together. All are articles that Rebekka Franck has written; all have errors in them that I have underlined.

Josephine is cooing satisfied from her playpen and I grab the phone and dial the newspaper again. This time I don't talk to the receptionist, this time I ask to talk to Rebekka Franck personally.

CHAPTER SIXTEEN

I INVITE her to come to my house for lunch. I tell her I have homemade sausages. She tells me it has been way too long and that she would love to swing by, but she is not going to be able to come until one thirty, is that okay?

"I have to finish this article I'm writing for tomorrow's paper," she says. "About the big house-fire yesterday. Maybe you've heard about it. A sixteen-year-old girl was killed. Real tragic. They think she was sleeping inside of the house when it happened. She was burnt beyond recognition. The parents told the police she was there and they found only a few body parts that they used to ID her by using DNA. That's what the article is about tomorrow." Rebekka paused. "I'm sorry if I'm grossing you out by telling too many details. It comes with the job. You get numb in the end."

"I heard about the fire," I say. "I was there. I killed the girl and set the house on fire afterwards."

A silence on the phone. I hear Rebekka talk to someone. Then she's back. "I'm sorry, that was my photographer. What did you say?"

"I said I hope you like sausages."

"Are you kidding? I love homemade sausages. Besides I'm looking forward to seeing you again. What has it been two years?"

"Two years, three months and seven days."

Rebekka laughs in the other end. "You always were funny," she says.

I don't laugh. I stare at the pile of newspaper clips with all the errors underlined.

"Can't wait to catch up," she says.

I pick up my kitchen-knife from the table. I have polished and sharpened it.

"Me either," I say.

Then we hang up. I walk into the living room and pick up Josephine. Then I feed her while fantasizing about cutting off Rebekka Franck's tongue.

When Josephine has fallen asleep I put her in the crib upstairs while thinking about where it would be best to kill Rebekka Franck. In the living room or maybe the kitchen since it's easier to clean. I'm thinking about doing it in the garage that I could arrange first with newspapers to make sure it didn't stain the floors. I walk out there, and realize that I'll have to move the car first. So I open the garage door and back into the driveway. Then I walk back and close the garage door. The room seems perfect now, I think. I move Jacob's bike and some plastic bags with his old toys. I tip one over and a pink, organic, non-toxic teddy bear falls out. I pick it up feeling my heart race in my chest. Who threw away Pinkie-Bear? I wonder. It is Josephine's favorite. Following an eerie feeling I empty the bag onto the garage floor. More toys. All baby toys, girl stuff, things I have been looking for. I go through it frantically, almost panicking. *What is all this stuff doing out here where Josephine can't play with it?* I don't understand. It seems so cruel somehow. I pick it up and bring it upstairs to the nursery. I throw everything in a pile, thinking I don't have time to put it up on the shelves now, but will do it later. I look at Josephine while she is sleeping. Suddenly she looks so pale, I think. My heart is pounding when I put my hand on her chest. It's moving, she's still breathing. I wonder why she is so pale all of a sudden and worry if she might be coming down with something. I decide to leave her alone to get some sleep and take the baby alarm with me downstairs. I spread out all the newspapers to cover the floor in the garage. I can't seem to get them to stay down, the papers keep moving every time I turn my back on them. I find the duct tape and tape them all to the floor so they won't move again. Sweating I walk back into the kitchen. The smell is back, I think and smell myself. I have to go upstairs and take another shower and get clean clothes on. I decide to wear a dress this time, since I am so hot. I dry my hair and put on make-up, then storm into the kitchen and begin preparing the sausages. I take out a bag from the new freezer and catch a look from Mr. Berendsen as I close the lid. I run into the kitchen and throw all the sausages into a pan, cover them in oil, then turn on the heat. I stare at the sausages roasting while I feel sweat running across my face. I look down at my dress and realize it's soaked in my sweat. It's dripping on my feet soaking my shoes as well. I look at the clock on the oven and realize I only have a few minutes. No time for a shower, I think and wipe the sweat off with a towel. It's soaked when I'm done. I smell my armpit and realize I stink. I don't have time to take care of it so I go to the sink and splash water on my face to wash it off. The sausages are roasting in the pan and soon the smell from them exceeds the smell of my sweat. At least I hope it does. I wipe my face again when I hear the doorbell ring.

CHAPTER SEVENTEEN

"**Y**OU LOOK wonderful, Lisa," Rebekka says when I open the door. She is holding a bouquet of flowers that she hands to me. I take it with a smile and tell her she looks great too, then walk to the kitchen while keeping a close look at all the aphids I see crawling on the leaves. I try to wash them off, but they seem to be stuck on it, so I decide to pretend they're not there until I have killed Rebekka, then I can throw the flowers out. There is no need to be rude, I think and smile at Rebekka as she enters the kitchen and I am put the flowers in a glass vase from the Danish luxury style-brand Georg Jensen.

"So how have you been?" she asks.

I turn my head like an owl to look at her. "Fine," I say while fighting the tic that has come back. I draw in a deep breath to keep me calm. "Just fine."

"I'm so glad to hear that," Rebekka says. She walks to the stove and looks at the sausages. "Um, smells delicious," she says.

I smile again, while grabbing the knife in my hand. I begin cutting salad and put it in a big bowl. The lumps are too big, but I don't care. I hardly look at it. I cut tomatoes, bell peppers and put in sunflower seeds. Rebekka is walking around looking at the kitchen.

"I'm so glad you called," she says. "I mean I've been wanting to stop by so many times, and thought about calling you a lot, but ... well you know, life got in the way, I guess."

I'm chopping rapidly now. The newspaper clippings on the counter are laughing at me. I'm sweating heavily, big drops are falling into the salad.

"Are you sure you're alright?" Rebekka asks.

"I'm great. Why shouldn't I be?"

Rebekka shrugs. "I don't know ... I guess ... well I just think that I would be devastated ..."

I interrupt her. "Sausages are done," I say and take them off the stove.

"Smells great," she says.

"You already said that," I correct her.

She pauses, I can tell she is startled. "I guess I just did," she says.

I poke the tip of the knife into the wooden carving board with a loud sound. Rebekka jumps and looks at me.

"That's just it," I say.

"What is? Are you sure you're okay? You seem a little ... well a little off to be frank."

I pull up the knife and hold it in front of me. "The problem is, Rebekka Franck, that I cannot keep quiet any longer. People make mistakes all the time, and those people need to know that what they are doing is WRONG!"

I'm yelling the last word and it frightens Rebekka. She jumps backwards while I walk towards her with the knife in my hand. "All those mistakes," I say. "All those errors. Couldn't you just have corrected them? Why did you keep on doing them? Why don't you take pride in what you do enough to do it properly? Don't you have any RESPECT for your readers?"

"Lisa. I don't know what you're talking about. To be honest you're kind of scaring me right now. I thought this was a friendly visit. I thought we were just talking, catching up. I can leave if you don't want me here."

I stomp my feet. Rebekka jumps again. "But I do want you here. How else can I correct you? I have been trying so hard to tell you about all the grammatical errors and typos in your articles, but that STUPID, PUTRID BITCH working on your newspaper doesn't seem to do anything about it. Why is that? Why don't you want to change it, Rebekka?"

"Wait. Are you the woman who has been calling us and telling us that we're making mistakes that we can't find anywhere? Is that you, Lisa?"

I stomp my feet again with the knife clenched in my hand. "Why won't you listen to me!" I say.

Rebekka shakes her head and puts her hand out. "Easy with the knife, Lisa. I'm sorry. I didn't know it was you who called. If you had told them it was you, I would have talked to you in person."

"But that's not the point, is it?" I say. The room is spinning and sweat is running across my face, dripping on the floor, soaking my clothes and leaving a puddle underneath my feet.

"I don't know," Rebekka answers. "You tell me. You tell me what the point is. Cause I don't seem to understand anything right now."

"The point is that everybody is so terribly WRONG. They do the wrong things all the time, why won't anyone do what is right for a change? Why doesn't anyone try and be the best they can be? Why doesn't anyone do their jobs properly anymore? Why don't doctors know when a baby is about to die? Why can't they tell when a baby is going to die? Why do they tell you it's healthy and then it dies overnight? Why don't they warn you, Rebekka?"

Rebekka stares at me. The knife is shivering in my hand. "Why Rebekka? Why?"

She shakes her head. "I don't know, Lisa. I don't know."

A terrifying feeling grabs me and I run upstairs. I storm into the nursery. My heart stops. The crib is empty. I let out a scream and fall to my knees, crying, yelling. I hear steps on the stairs, Rebekka is behind me now. I feel her hand on my shoulder. "I'm so, so sorry," she says with a low voice.

"I can't find my baby," I mumble between breaths. "Someone has taken my baby." For a second I wonder if it's the neighbor again, but I don't move. I cover my face with my hands and cry.

"I'm so sorry for your loss," Rebekka says. "It has to be the worst thing in the world to lose your child only three days after giving birth. I can't even imagine how hard it has to be."

I'm hyperventilating now. The knife is still clenched in my hand. It get up and point the knife at Rebekka. "I have to kill you now," I say.

Rebekka looks at me compassionately. She's not even afraid. It surprises me. "I understand your anger," she says. "I think I would want to kill the entire world too."

"But I will. I will kill you," I say. "Like I killed all those other people. I murdered them, Rebekka. I really did."

Rebekka walks closer. She pushes the knife to the side, then grabs me and hugs me tight. "Oh you silly head," she says. "You couldn't kill a fly if you tried to. Don't you think I know you? We've been friends for twenty-five years."

"But you don't know what I've done. I have killed many people. I really have, Rebekka."

She shakes her head with a smile. "I don't think you have.

I don't know what's going on with you, and I didn't want to tell you this, but I talked to your husband earlier today to make sure it wasn't too much for you to have me over for lunch today and he told me you have been very sick for a long time, but you're slowly getting better now. Grief is a horrible thing. It messes with your brain causing you to imagine all kinds of stuff. Christian told me you have hardly slept ever since it happened, that you never eat, that you've had a hard time letting go of Josephine and that he had to remove her stuff slowly and one toy at a time when you weren't looking. He also told me that you have been walking around with the empty baby carriage day and night. I think your mind has been messing with you. You might have imagined killing someone, but you have never done such an awful thing. I simply can't believe it."

"But I did. The girl, the one who died in the fire yesterday. That was me. I killed her with this knife."

"No you didn't. She died in the fire. It was tragic, yes, but it wasn't murder. I talked to the police about it yesterday. It was an accident caused by a leak in the gas for the stove. End of story. Your mind is playing tricks on you."

"But I know that I'm a killer."

"How ..?

I drop the knife on the floor. It doesn't make a sound when it hits the soft carpet. "Because I killed my baby. She ... she was on her stomach when I found her." I am crying heavily now. I can't seem to get my brain to keep still. I can't focus. My sight is blurry. All I see is blood. Blood running down the walls, blood on the floors, blood flushing from the crib.

"What have I done?" I ask and look at Rebekka. Her face is covered in blood. It's flushing down her face. "I killed my baby."

Rebekka grabs my hands and take them in hers. She looks at me with compassion. "You can't do this to yourself, Lisa," she says. "It wasn't your fault. Sometimes babies just die."

The sentence keeps echoing in my head. I want it to stop. *Sometimes babies just die. Sometimes babies just die.*

"It wasn't your fault," she repeats. "You did everything right. You can't keep blaming yourself, or you'll lose it. You need to stay strong for your family. For your children. For Jacob and Amalie. They all need you. Even Christian needs you."

I'm crying heavily now, throwing myself in Rebekka's arms. She's holding me tight. I have a pain in my stomach that won't go away.

"I think we better get you out of here," Rebekka says. "Let me take you to see your doctor. He can get you the help you need."

I'm crying and nodding. I sob, sniffle and look at the crib. It's still empty, even the blood is gone. "I think I might like that," I say. "I think I need help."

"Of course you do. No one should go through a thing like this all alone. You need to talk to a professional before you lose complete touch with reality."

Rebekka helps me get down the stairs. I feel a pinch in the heart when I realize the playpen is gone. It knocks the breath out of me. I look into the kitchen where the sausages are on the counter.

"Leave them. Let's go see your doctor, then grab a late lunch at a café afterwards, okay?"

I smile and nod. "Let me just clean the mess up," I say.

I go to the kitchen and take out a roll of aluminum foil. I put all the sausages in the foil and wrap them up. I put the pan in the sink and then walk down to the freezer in the basement.

I open the lid and put the sausages in for later. I push Mr. Berendsen's head to the side to make more room. I feel like he stares at me when I close the lid.

"Be right there," I yell before I run up the stairs and shut the light off on my way up.

THE END

AFTERWORD

Dear Reader,

Thank you for purchasing *Rock-a-bye-baby*. I hope you enjoyed it. This is a short story that is part of a collection of short stories from the Danish town of Karrebaeksminde. Get the entire collection or get the stories separately by following the links below.

Karrebaeksminde is also the town where my horror-series, the Rebekka Franck-series takes place beginning with the first book *One, Two ... He is coming for you*. I have put in an excerpt from the first book on the following pages.

Take care,
Willow

- There's No Place like Home
- Slenderman
- Where the Wild Roses Grow

JACK RYDER SERIES

- Hit the Road Jack
- Slip out the Back Jack
- The House that Jack Built
- Black Jack

REBEKKA FRANCK SERIES

- One, Two...He is Coming for You
- Three, Four...Better Lock Your Door
- Five, Six...Grab your Crucifix
- Seven, Eight...Gonna Stay up Late
- Nine, Ten...Never Sleep Again
- Eleven, Twelve...Dig and Delve
- Thirteen, Fourteen...Little Boy Unseen

HORROR SHORT-STORIES

- Better watch out
- Eenie, Meenie
- Rock-a-Bye Baby

- Nibble, Nibble, Crunch
- Humpty Dumpty
- Chain Letter

PARANORMAL SUSPENSE/FANTASY NOVELS

AFTERLIFE SERIES

- Beyond
- Serenity
- Endurance
- Courageous

THE WOLFBOY CHRONICLES

- A Gypsy Song
- I am WOLF

DAUGHTERS OF THE JAGUAR

- Savage
- Broken

ABOUT THE AUTHOR

 The Queen of scream novels Willow Rose is an international best-selling author. She writes Mystery/Suspense/Horror, Paranormal Romance and Fantasy. She is inspired by authors like James Patterson, Agatha Christie, Stephen King, Anne Rice, and Isabel Allende. She lives on Florida's Space Coast with her husband and two daughters. When she is not writing or reading, you'll find her surfing and watching the dolphins play in the waves of the Atlantic Ocean. She has sold more than two million books.

Connect with Willow online:

willow-rose.net
madamewillowrose@gmail.com

ONE, TWO... HE'S COMING FOR YOU

EXCERPT

For a special sneak peak of Willow Rose's Bestselling Mystery Novel ***One, Two... He's Coming for You (Rebekka Franck #1)*** turn to the next page.

———

One, two, He is coming for you.
Three, four, better lock your door.
Five, six, grab your crucifix.
Seven, eight, gonna stay up late.
Nine, ten, you will never sleep again.

———

ONE, TWO... HE IS COMING FOR YOU

REBEKKA FRANCK #1

PROLOGUE

ONE, TWO... the song in his head wouldn't escape. Sure, he knew where it came from. It was that rhyme from the horror movies. The ones with the serial killer, that Freddy Krueger guy with a burned, disfigured face, red and dark green striped sweater, brown fedora hat, and a glove armed with razors to kill his victims in their dreams and take their souls, which would kill them in the real world. "A Nightmare on Elm Street," that was the movie's name. Yes, he knew its origin. And he had his reasons for singing that particular song in this exact moment. He knew why, and so would his future victims.

He lit a cigarette and stared out the window at a waiting bird in the bare treetop. Waiting for the sunlight to come back, just like the rest of the kingdom of Denmark at this time of the year. Waiting for spring with its explosion of colors, like a sea of promises of sunlight and a warmer wind. But still the winter had to go away. And it hadn't. The trees were still naked, the sky gray as steel, the ground wet and cold. February always seemed the longest month in the little country though it was the shortest in the calendar. People talked about it every day as they showed up for work or school.

Every freaking day since Christmas.

Now, it wouldn't be long before the light came back. But in reality it always took months of waiting and anticipating before spring finally appeared.

The man staring out the window didn't pay much attention to the weather though. He stood with his cigarette between two fingers. To him, the time he had been waiting ages for was finally here.

He kept humming the same song, the same line. *One, two, he is coming for you* .... The cigarette burned a hole in the parquet floor. He picked up the remains with his hands wearing white plastic gloves and carefully placed them in a small plastic bag that he put in his brown briefcase. He would leave no trace of being in the house where the body of another man was soon to be found.

He closed the briefcase and went into the hall, where he sat in a leather chair by the door to the main entrance.

Waiting for his victim to come home.

He glanced at himself in the mirror by the entrance door. He could see from where he was sitting how nicely he had dressed for the occasion.

He was outfitted in a blue blazer with the famous Trolle coat of arms on the chest, little yellow emblem with a red headless lion—the traditional blazer for a student of Herlufsholm boarding school. The school was located by the Susaa River in Naestved, about 80 kilometers south of Copenhagen, the capital of Denmark. As the oldest boarding school in Denmark, the school took pride in an array of unique traditions. Some of them the world outside never would want to know about.

The blazer was now too small, so he couldn't close it, but

otherwise he was looking almost like he had been back in 1986. He was, after all, still a fairly handsome man. And unlike the majority of the guys from back then, he had kept most of his hair.

His victim had done well for himself, he noticed. No surprise in that though, with parents who were multibillionaires. The old villa by the sea of Smaalands farvandet in the southern part of Zeeland was big and admirable. It could easily fit a couple of families. It was typical of his victim to have a place like this just as his holiday residence.

When he heard the Jaguar on the gravel outside, he took the glove out of the briefcase and put it on his right hand. He stretched his fingers and the metal claws followed.

He listened for voices but didn't hear any to his satisfaction.

His victim was alone.

CHAPTER ONE

"**W**E'RE GOING to be too late. Do you want me to be fired on my first day"? I yelled for the third time while gazing up the stairs for my six-year-old daughter, Julie.

"Go easy on her, Rebekka. It's her first day too," argued my father.

He stood in the doorway to the living room of my childhood home, leaning on his cane. I smiled to myself. How I had missed him all these years living in the other part of the country. Now he had gotten old, and I felt like I had missed out on so much and that he had missed out on so much of our lives too. It was fifteen years since I left the town to study journalism. I had only been back a few times since and then, of course, when Mom died five years ago. Why didn't I visit him more often, especially after he was alone? Instead I had left it to my sister to take care of him. She lived in Naestved about fifteen minutes away.

Well there was no point in wondering now.

"You can't change the past," my dad would say. And did

say when I called him crying my heart out and asking him if Julie and I could come and stay with him for a while.

I sighed and wished I could change the past and change everything about my past. Except for one thing. One delightful little blond thing.

"I'm ready, Mom."

Her.

Julie is the love of my life. Everything I've done has been for her and her future. I sacrificed everything to give her a better life. But that meant I had to leave it all behind—her dad, our friends and neighbors, and my career with a huge salary. All for her.

"I'm ready." She ran down the stairs looking like an angel with her beautiful blond hair braided in the back.

"Yes, you are," I nodded and looked into her bright blue eyes. "Do you have everything ready for school"?

She sighed with annoyance and walked past me.

"Are you coming or not?" She asked when she reached the door.

I picked up my bag from the floor, kissed my dad on the cheek, and followed my daughter who waited impatiently.

"After you my dear," I said as we left the house.

I found a job at a local newspaper in Karrebaeksminde. It wasn't much of a promotion since I used to work for one of the biggest newspapers in the country. *Jyllandsposten* was located in Aarhus, the second biggest town in Denmark. That was where we used to live.

When I had a family.

I used to be their star reporter, one of those who always gets the cover stories. Moving back to my childhood town was not an easy choice, since I knew I had to give up my position as a well-known reporter. But it had to be done. I had to get away.

Now, after dropping off my daughter at her new school and smoking two cigarettes in anxiety for my daughter's first day, I found myself at my new workplace.

"You must be Rebekka Franck. Welcome to our editorial room," said a sweet elderly lady sitting at one of the two desks piled high with stacks of paper. I looked around the room and saw no one else. The room was a mess, and so was she. Her long red hair went in all directions. She had tried to tame it with a butterfly hair clip, but it didn't seem to do the job. She got up and waddled her chubby body in a flowered yellow dress over to greet me.

"I'm Sara," she said. "I'm in charge of all the personal pages. You know, the obituaries and such. People come to me if they need to put in an announcement for a reception or a 50-year anniversary celebration. Stuff like that. That's what I do."

I nodded and looked confused at all the old newspapers in stacks on the floor.

"You probably would like to see your desk."

I nodded again and smiled kindly. "Yes, please."

"It's right over there." Sara pointed at the other desk in the room. Then she looked back at me, smiling widely. "It's just going to be the two of us."

I smiled back, a little scared of the huge possibility of going insane in the near future. I knew it was a small newspaper that covered all of Zeeland, and that this would only be the department taking care of the local news from Karrebaeksminde. But still ... two people. Could that be all?

"Do you want to see the rest of your new workplace?" Sara asked and I nodded.

She took a couple of steps to the right and opened a door. "In here we have a small kitchen with a coffeemaker and the bathroom."

"Let me guess. That's it?" I tried not to sound too sarcastic. This was really a step down for me, to put it mildly.

Sara sat down and put on a set of headphones. I moved a stack of newspapers and found my chair underneath. I opened my laptop and up came a picture of Julie, me, and her dad on our trip to Sharm el-Sheikh in Egypt. We all wore goggles and big smiles. Quickly I closed the lid of the laptop and closed my eyes.

Damn him, I thought. Damn that stupid moron.

I got up from the desk and went into the break room to grab a cup of coffee. I opened the window and lit a cigarette. For several minutes I stared down at the street. A few people rushed by. Otherwise it was a sleepy town compared to where I used to live. I thought about my husband and returning to Aarhus, but that was simply not an option for me. I had to make it here.

I drank the rest of the coffee and killed my cigarette on the bottom of the mug. Then I closed the window and stepped back into the editorial room.

I need to clean this place up, I thought but then regretted the idea. It was simply too much work for one person for now. Maybe another day. Maybe I could persuade Sara to help me. I looked at her with the gigantic headphones on her ears. It made her face look even fatter. It was too bad that she was so overweight. She actually had a pretty face and attractive brown eyes. She looked at me and took off the headphones.

"What are you listening to?" I asked and expected that it was a radio station or a CD of her favorite music. But it wasn't.

"It's a police scanner," she said.

I looked at her surprised. "You have a police scanner?"

She nodded.

"I thought police everywhere in the country had shifted from traditional radio-scanners to using a digital system."

"Maybe in your big city, but down here we still use the old-fashioned ones."

"What do you use it for?"

"It is the best way to keep track of what is happening in this town. I get my best stories to tell my neighbors from this little fellow," she said while she leaned over gave the radio a friendly tap. "We originally got this baby for journalistic purposes, in order to be there when a story breaks, like a bank has been robbed or something like that. But the past five or six years nothing much has happened in our town, so it hasn't brought any stories to the newspaper. But I sure have a lot of fun listening to it."

She leaned over her desk with excitement in her brown eyes.

"Like the time when the mayor's wife got caught drunk in her car. That was great. Or when the police were called out to a domestic dispute between the pastor and his wife. As it turned out she had been cheating on him. Now that was awesome."

I stared at the woman in front of me and didn't know exactly what to say. Instead I just smiled and started walking back to my desk, when she stopped me.

"Ah, yes I forgot. We are not all alone. We do have a photographer working here too. He only comes in when there's a job for him to do. His name is Sune Johansen. He looks a little weird, but you'll learn to love him. He's from a big city too."

CHAPTER TWO

DIDRIK ROSENFELDT thought of a lot of things when he got out of the car and went up the stairs to his summer residence. He thought about the day he just had. The board meeting in his investment company went very well. He fired 3000 people in his windmill company early in the afternoon without even blinking. The hot young secretary gave him a blow job in his office afterwards. He thought about his annoying wife who kept calling him all afternoon. She was having a charity event this upcoming Saturday and kept bothering him with stupid details, as if she would ever be sober enough to go through it. Didn't she know by now that he was too busy to deal with that kind of stuff? He was humming when he reached the door to the house by the sea.

A tune ran through his head, his favorite song since he was a kid. "Money makes the world go round. A mark, a yen, a buck, or a pound. That clinking clanking sound can make the world go 'round." Didrik sighed and glanced back at his shiny new silver Jaguar. Money did indeed make the world go around. And so did he.

A lot of thoughts flitted through Didrik's head when he

put the key in the old hand-carved wooden door and opened it. But death was not one of them.

"You!" was his only word when his eyes met the ones belonging to a guy he remembered from school. A boy really, he always thought of him. The boy had nerve to be sitting in his new leather chair—"The Egg" designed by Arne Jacobsen—and wearing his despicable grubby old blazer from the boarding school. The boy was about to make a complete fool of himself. Didrik shut the door behind him with a bang.

"What do you want"? He placed his briefcase on the floor, took off his long black coat and hung it on a hanger in the entrance closet. He sighed and looked at the man with pity.

"So"?

All the girls at Herlufsholm boarding school had whispered about the boy when he first arrived there in ninth grade. Unlike most of the rich high-society boys, including Didrik Rosenfeldt who was both fat and red headed, the boy was a handsome guy. He had nice brown hair and the most sparkling blue eyes. He was tall and the hard work he used to do at his dad's farm outside of Naestved had made him strong and muscular and Didrik and his friends soon noticed that the girls liked that ... a lot.

The boy wasn't rich like the rest of them. In fact his parents had no money. But in a strange way that made him exotic to the girls. The poor countryside boy, the handsome stranger from a different culture who might take them away from their boring rich lives. They thought he could rescue them from ending up like their rich drunk mothers. How his parents were able to afford the extremely expensive school, no one knew. Some said he was there because his mother used to do it with the headmaster, but Didrik knew that wasn't true. This boy's family was—unlike everybody else's at the school—hardworking, earnest people. The kind who people like Didrik had no respect for whatsoever, the kind his father would exploit and then throw away. He and his type were expendable. They were workers. And that made it even more fun to pretend he would be the boy's friend.

Despite that he was younger than they were, they had from time to time accepted him as their equal in the brotherhood.

But because of his background he would always fall through. And they would laugh at him behind his back, even sometimes to his face. Like the time when they were skeet shooting on Kragerup Estate, and Didrik put a live cat in the catapult. Boy, they had their fun telling that story for weeks after. How the poor pretty boy had screamed, when he shot the kitty and it fell bleeding to the ground. What a wimp.

"So, what do you want? Can't you even say anything? Are you that afraid of me?" Didrik said arrogantly.

The pretty boy stood up from the $7000 chair and took a step toward him, his right hand hidden behind his back. Didrik sighed again. He was sick and tired of this game. It led nowhere and he was wasting his time. Didrik was longing to get into his living room and get a glass of the fine $900 cognac he just imported from France. He was not going to let a stupid poor boy from his past get in the way of that. That was for certain. He loosened his tie and looked with aggravation at the boy in front of him.

"How did you even get in here?"

"Smashed a window in the back."

Didrik snorted. Now he would have to go through the trouble to get someone out here to fix it tonight.

"Just tell me what you want, boy."

The pretty blue eyes stared at him.

"You know exactly what I want."

Didrik sighed again. Enough with these games! Until now he had been patient with this guy. But now he was about to feel the real Rosenfeldt anger. The same anger Didrik's dad used to show when Didrik's mother brought him into his study and he would beat Didrik half to death with a fire poker. The same anger that his dad used to show the world that it was the Rosenfeldts who made the decisions. Everybody obeyed their rules because they had the money and the power.

"You're making a fool of yourself. Just get out of here before I call someone to get rid of you. I'm a very powerful man, you know. I can have you killed just by pressing a number on my phone," he said taking out a black iPhone from his pocket.

"I know very well how powerful you and your family are. But we are far away from your thugs; and I will have killed you by the time they get here."

Didrik put the phone back in his pocket. He now sensed the boy was more serious than he first anticipated.

"Do you want to kill me? Is that it?"

"Yes."

Didrik laughed out loud. It echoed in the hall. The boy did not seem intimidated. That frightened him.

"Don't be ridiculous. You are such a fool. A complete idiot. You always were." Didrik snorted. "Look at you. You look like a homeless person in that old school blazer. Your clothes are all dirty. And when did you last shave? What happened to you?"

"You did. You and your friends. You ruined my life."

Didrik laughed again. This time not nearly as loud and confident.

"Is it that old thing you are still sobbing about?"

"How could I not be?"

"Come on. It happened twenty-five years ago. Christ, I didn't even come up with the idea." Didrik snorted again. "Pah! You wouldn't dare to kill me. Remember I am a nobleman and you are nothing but a peasant who tried to be one of us for a little while. You can take the boy away from the farm but you can't take the farm out of the boy. You have always been nothing but a stupid little farmer boy."

Didrik watched the boy lift his right hand, revealing a thing from his past, something he couldn't forget. With a wild expression in his eyes, he then moved the blades of the glove and took two steps in Didrik's direction with them all pointing at him. . It scared the shit out of him. It had been years since he last saw the glove and thought it had been lost. But the pretty boy had found it. Now the game was in the boy's court.

"I can give you money." Desperately, he clung to what normally saved him in troubled times. "Is it money you want? I could call my secretary right now and make a transfer."

He took out the iPhone again.

"I could give you a million. Would that be enough? Two million? You could buy yourself a nice house, maybe get some nice new clothes, and buy a new car."

The boy in front of him finally smiled showing his beautiful bright teeth. Phew! Money had once again saved him. At least he thought. But only for a second.

"I don't want your blood money."

Didrik didn't understand. Who in the world would say no to money? "But ..."

"I told you. I want you dead. I want you to suffer just as I have been for twenty-five years. I want you to be humiliated like I was."

Didrik sighed deeply. "But why now?"

"Because your time has run out."

"I don't understand."

The boy with the pretty blue eyes stepped closer and now stood face to face with Didrik. The four claws on his hand were all pointing towards Didrik's head. The boy's eyes were cold as ice, when he said the words that made everything inside Didrik Rosenfeldt shiver: "The game is over."

CHAPTER THREE

L ARI SOERENSEN enjoyed her job as a housekeeper for
the Rosenfeldt family. Not that she liked Mr. Rosenfeldt in particular but she liked taking care of his summer
residence by the sea. They barely ever used it, only for a few
weeks in the summer and whenever Mr. Rosenfeldt had one
of his affairs with a local waitress or his secretary. He would
escape to the house in Karrebaeksminde for "a little privacy"
as he called it.

But otherwise there wasn't much work in keeping the
house clean, and Lari Soerensen could do it at her own pace.
She would turn on the music in the living room and sing
while she polished the parquet floor. She would eat of the
big box of chocolate in the kitchen. She would take the
money in the ashtrays and the coins lying on the shelves and
put it in her pocket knowing the family would never miss it.
Sometimes she would even use the phone to call her mother
in the Philippines, which normally was much too expensive
for her. Her Danish husband didn't want to pay for her
phone calls to her family anymore, and since he took all the

money she got from cleaning people's houses, she couldn't pay for the calls herself.

It was a cold but lovely morning as she walked pass the port and glanced at all the yachts that would soon be put back in the water when spring arrived. All the rich people would go sailing and drinking on their big boats.

She took in a breath of the fresh morning air. She had three houses to clean today and she would begin with Mr. Rosenfeldt's since he probably wouldn't be there. It was only five thirty, and the city had barely awakened. Everything was so quiet, not even a car.

She had taken a lot of time to get used to living in the little kingdom of Denmark. Being from the Philippines, she was used to a warmer climate and people in her homeland were a lot more open and friendly than what she experienced here. Not that they were not nice to her—they were. But it was hard for her to get accustomed to the fact that people didn't speak to you if they didn't know you. If she would talk to a woman in the supermarket she would answer briefly and without looking at Lari. It wasn't impolite; it was custom. People were busy and had enough in themselves.

But once people got to know somebody they would be very friendly. They wouldn't necessarily stop and talk if they met in the street. Often they were way too busy for that, but they would smile. And Lari would smile back, feeling accepted in the small community. If people became friends with someone they might even invite them to dinner and would get very drunk, and then the Danes wouldn't stop talking until it was early in the morning. They would tell a lot of jokes and laugh a lot. They had a strange sense of humor that she had to get used to. They used sarcasm all the time, and she had a hard time figuring out when they actually meant what they said or when they were just joking.

CHAPTER FOUR

I **AWOKE** feeling like I was lying under a strange comforter in a foreign place in an unknown city. Slowly my memory came back to me, when I looked at my sleeping daughter in the bed next to me. When I came home from work she told me the first day of school had been a little tough. The teachers were nice, but the other kids in the class didn't want to talk to her and she had spent the day alone and made no new friends. I told her she would be fine, that it would soon be better, but inside I was hurting. This was supposed to be a fresh start for the both of us, a new beginning. I now realized it wouldn't go as smoothly as I had hoped.

My dad had prepared a nice breakfast for us when we came downstairs. Coffee, toast and eggs. Soft boiled for me and scrambled for Julie. We dove into the food.

Before mom died he wouldn't go near the kitchen, except to eat, but things had changed since then. *He's actually gotten pretty good at cooking*, I thought while secretly observing him from the table. Ever since his fall down the

But Lari liked that they laughed so much. She did too. Smiled and laughed. That's how she got by during the day, the month, the year. That's what she did when the rich white man from Denmark came to her house in the Philippines and told her mother, that he wanted to marry Lari and take her back to Denmark and pay the family a lot of money for her. That's what she did when she signed the paperwork and they were declared married and she knew her future was saved. She smiled when she got on the plane with her ugly white husband who wore clogs and dirty overalls. She even smiled when he showed her into the small messy house that hadn't been cleaned for ages and told her that was her new home. That her job would be to cook and clean and be available to him at any time. She was still smiling, even at the end of the day when she handed over the money that she earned from housecleaning while her husband sat at home and was paid by the government to be unemployed. And when Mr. Rosenfeldt grabbed her and took her into his bed and had oral sex with her she still smiled.

Yes, Lari Soerensen always smiled. And she still did today when she unlocked the door to Mr. Rosenfeldt's summer residence.

But from that moment on she would smile no more.

stairs last year, he had to use a cane, but he still managed to get around the kitchen and cook for us.

"You know, Dad, with me in the house you could catch a break every once in a while. I could take care of you, and cook for you instead."

He didn't even turn around, but just snorted at me. "I know my way around. You would only mess the place up."

Then he turned around, smiling at Julie and me, and placed a big plate of scrambled eggs on the table in front of us.

I sighed and rubbed my stomach.

"Sorry, Dad, I'm too full. Julie, go get your bag upstairs. We are leaving in five."

Julie made an annoyed sound and rushed up the stairs.

My dad looked at me seriously.

"She misses him, you know," he said nodding his head in Julie's direction. "Isn't it about time she got to call him, and talk to him?"

I shook my head. I hated that she had told her granddad she missed her father. Since I couldn't leave my job until late in the afternoon, he had suggested he would pick her up every day and they could spend some quality grandpa-grand-daughter time together catching up on all the years they missed of each others' lives. I liked that, but I didn't care much about him meddling in my life.

"I can't have him knowing where we are."

My dad sighed. "You can't hide down here forever. If he wants to find you, he will. Whatever happened to you up there, you have to face it at one point. You can't keep running from it. It will affect your daughter too. No matter what he did, he is, after all, still her dad."

Now it was my turn to sigh. "Just not right now, okay?"

As I got up Julie came down and dumped her bag on the

floor before sitting down again and taking another serving of eggs.

Where she would put it in her skinny little body I didn't know but I was glad to see her eat despite being so nervous about another day alone in the schoolyard with no one to play with.

"She must be growing," my dad said with a big smile. "That's my girl," he said and winked at her.

I looked at the clock and decided that I too had the time to sit down for another minute. The radio played an old Danish song from my childhood. My dad started humming and tried to spin around with his cane. He almost fell but avoided it in the last second and we all laughed. I began to sing along too and Julie rolled her eyes at me, which made me sing even louder. The old cat stopped licking herself and stared at us from the window. She would probably be rolling her eyes too if she could.

It was one of those beautiful mornings, but a freezing cold one too. The sun embraced everybody, promising them that soon it would triumph over the cold wind. Soon it would make the flowers come out of hiding in the ground and with its long warm arms it would make them flourish and bloom. I really enjoyed my drive along the ocean and the sandy beach. The ocean seemed angry.

I had promised headquarters to do a story today, an interview with an Italian artist, Giovanni Marco, who lived on Enoe, a small island close to Karrebaeksminde. It was connected to the mainland by a bridge. The artist had made a series of sculptures that made the public angry because of its vulgarity. The artist himself claimed that it was his way of making a statement, that art cannot be censored. He had displayed the sculptures in the county's art festival, shocking the public and making people nauseous from looking at them.

He was the same artist who once had displayed ten blenders each with one goldfish in them in a museum of art, waiting to see if anyone in the audience would press the button and kill the fish. He loved to provoke the sleepy Danes and outrage them. At least they then took a position and cared about something. I remembered he said he wanted to wake them from their drowsy sleep walk. I was actually looking forward to this interview with this controversial man on the beautiful island.

Giovanni Marco lived in an old wooden beach house that looked like it wouldn't survive if big storm should hit the beach. Fortunately big storms are rare in Denmark. We had a big one in 1999 as strong as a category 1 hurricane. It was still the one people remembered and talked about. It knocked down trees and electric wires. At least one tree hit a moving car and killed the driver inside. That was a tragedy. It could definitely get very windy, but the artist's house would probably stand for another hundred years.

Barefooted, he welcomed me in the driveway with a hug and a kiss on my cheek, which overwhelmed me since I had not been happy about male physical contact lately. So I'm sure I came off stiff and probably not very friendly toward him.

He was gorgeous and he seemed to know that a little too well. I never liked men who thought too much of themselves, but this one intrigued me anyway, which made me nervous and uncomfortable in his presence.

His blue eyes stared at me while he invited me inside.

It's rare for an Italian man to have blue eyes like that, I thought. Maybe he had Scandinavian genes. Maybe that's why he had escaped from sunny Italy to cold Denmark where the sun would hide all winter. His hair was thick and brown and his skin looked very Italian. But he was tall like a Scandinavian. And muscular. I hated to admit it, but it was attractive.

Inside I was stunned by the spectacular view from almost every room in the house: views of the raging ocean, of the wild and absorbing sea. I used to dream about living like that. Well I used to dream about a lot of things, but dreams have a tendency to get broken over the years.

Giovanni, in a tank top and sweatpants, smiled at me and offered me a cup of organic green tea. I am more of a coffee person, but I smiled graciously and accepted. We sat for awhile on his sofa, glancing out over the big ocean.

"So you have just returned from the big city?" he asked with an irresistible Italian accent. His Danish was good, but not as good as I expected. BI had read that he had lived in the country for more than 30 years. "What made you come back?"

News of my return traveled fast in a small community, I knew that, but how it got all the way out here, I didn't know. Overwhelmed by his directness I shook my head and said, "I missed the silence and the quiet days, I guess." It wasn't too far from the truth. There had been days in the end, when the city got to me, with all its smartass people drinking their Coffee "Lattes". It used to be just coffee with milk. I didn't get that. But then again I didn't get sushi either. Even in the center of Karrebaeksminde they had a sushi restaurant now, so maybe it wasn't a big city thing.

"I miss that too when I'm away from here." Giovanni expressed his emotions widely with his arms, the way Italians did. "Especially when I go back to Milan. I get so tired in the head, you know? All those people, so busy, always in a hurry. To do what? What are they doing that is so important?"

"I wouldn't know," I said knowing that I used to be one of those busy big-city people always rushing off to something. Rushing after a story to put on the cover. Never stopping to feel the ocean breeze or see the flowers pop up at spring. But I wasn't like that anymore. I had changed. Having to go off to cover the war for the newspaper had changed me. Being a mom changed me. But that was all history.

I began my interview with Giovanni Marco and got some pretty good statements, I thought. I began to see the article shape in my head. But it seemed more like he wanted to talk about me instead. He kept turning the conversation to me and my past. I didn't like to talk about it, so I gently avoided answering. But he kept pressing on, looking me in the eyes as if he could see right through me. I didn't like that and he began to annoy me. His constant flirting with me was a little over the top. Luckily, my cell phone started ringing just as he began asking about my husband.

"I better take this," I said.

"Now? In the middle of our conversation? Now, that is what I think is wrong with this world today. All these cell-phones always interrupting everything. People using them on the bus, on trains, in the doctor's waiting room, rambling about this and that, and playing games. God forbid they should ever get themselves into a real conversation. They might even risk getting to know someone outside their own little world."

He got up and looked passionately in my eyes, and I

couldn't help smiling. He was indeed over the top, but it was sweet.

"Now, tell me, what could be so vital that it cannot wait until we are done?" He thrust his long Italian arms out in the air.

"It might be about my daughter," I said and got up from the couch.

It wasn't about Julie. It was Sara from the newspaper. She was almost hyperventilating, trying to catch her breath. She was rambling.

"Take it easy Sara," I said while holding a finger in my other ear to better hear her. "Just tell me calmly what is going on."

She took a pause and caught her breath. "A dead body. The police found a dead body. I just heard it on my radio."

"So?"

"Are you kidding me? That's like the biggest story of this century down here."

I didn't get it. Normally when we received news like that at my old newspaper they just put in a small note on page five, and that was it. If the police thought it was a murder and an investigation took place we would make a real article about it, but still only place it on page five. And Sara didn't even know if it was considered to be a murder case or not. It was just a dead body. For all I knew he could have died of a heart attack.

"Don't people die in this place?" I challenged.

In Aarhus people died every week. With the gangs of immigrants fighting the rockers people got shot and stabbed all the time. Of course they would bring the story if a dead body was found. But it wasn't like it was one of the big ones.

"He might have fallen drunk or even had a heart attack," I said trying to close the conversation. "I will call the police and get something for a small article when I come back, okay?"

"No, no, no. It is not okay at all. I called Sune. He is already on his way down there. You have to be there before anyone else. I got this from the police radio, remember? That means no one else in the country knows anything yet. It is what you would call a solo story."

I liked the ring of that. I might get it on the cover of the morning paper. Not bad on my second day.

"Okay, give me the address."

CHAPTER FIVE

H ALF AN hour later, I arrived at the scene. As I got near the address, I immediately knew this was no heart attack or just a drunken man. Four police cars were parked in front of the same house, two of them called in from Naestved, the biggest city nearby. I recognized a big blue van as one the forensic team from Copenhagen used.

This was big stuff.

The entrance to the house was blocked by crime tape. On the other side of the tape policemen searched wearing suits and gloves, writing in their notebooks, marking trace evidence, dusting for fingerprints, and marking shoeprints.

According to the radio report Sara had heard on the scanner, the victim was a white male, 46 years old. But I already knew that when I got there. I recognized the house and knew that it could only be Didrik Rosenfeldt. The house used to belong to his parents when I was a kid. And Didrik would come down here on summer vacation from boarding school. He was my sister's age, and I remembered them hanging out together one summer. But something happened and she dumped him and never spoke of him again. He was a real asshole as far as I knew. He used to come down here and flirt with almost anything that had a pulse. He spent his time hanging out on his parent's yacht in the port, drinking with his friends from the boarding school, harassing people who were different than they and had less money. A real prick, I would call him. That probably hadn't changed a bit.

I looked around at the small crowd of neighborhood kids who had gathered in front of the house, peeking in. In the middle, a tall skinny guy stood out. He had a green Mohawk and wore a leather band with spikes around his neck, a leather jacket, and several piercings in his eyebrows, lips and nose. He wore black make-up on his eyes and lips. He stood out in stark contrast to this crowd of high society upper-class kids. In his hands he held a camera that never left his eyes, constantly taking a series of pictures. As I got close to him I noticed that he was missing two of his fingers on his right hand.

"You must be Sune," I said when I approached him.

He didn't look down at me, just kept on taking pictures non-stop.

"Mmm ..."

"I'm Rebekka Franck. Did you see anything yet?"

"Nope."

"Has the body been taken out yet?"

"Nope."

Great, I thought. Then there was a chance we could get a picture of the covered body on the way into the ambulance. That was always a good shot for an article of this kind.

"Don't you think it's weird, since the body was found at six o'clock this morning?" Sune asked me.

Now that he said it, I did. It was three in the afternoon. Weren't they in a hurry to get the body to the lab right away and find the cause of death?

"Yeah, what does that mean?"

"That the body has been hard to get out. Maybe it was lying under something or was tied to something."

I nodded. This guy knew how to use his head. Not many could do that these days without getting hurt.

"Sounds likely."

"It must at least be a messy crime scene since it has taken them so long. There are a lot of people in there."

I nodded again. This guy had been at a crime scene before. And it probably wasn't here in Karrebaeksminde where he got that kind of experience.

"You're not from around here, are you?" I asked.

"Nope."

"Copenhagen?"

"Christiania. Have been and always will be a Christianite."

Ah, a free spirit from Christiania. Also known as "fristaden," the free-state. It was an area in Copenhagen that had around a thousand inhabitants. They lived by what they liked to call a collectivistic anarchy. Some called it a socialist anarchy. It meant that everybody living there got to take part in all the decisions. To the Christianites, as they called themselves, it meant they were different from the rest of the society and that they lived by their own rules. To the rest of the world it meant that this was a place you could go and buy pot on the streets of Christiania where they sold it out in the open even if it was illegal in the rest of the country. They were a state within the state that the police didn't touch. They even had their own flag, red with three yellow dots. Today things had changed though. The liberal government had sent in the police and tried to fight the illegal drug trade, and they wanted to remove all the houses that the Christianites had build themselves.

My guess was that Sune wasn't too thrilled about the police in general. I guessed right.

I kept a close eye on the activities behind the crime-scene tape and soon I spotted the detective who seemed to be in charge. He came out of the house and headed towards one of the police cars, and I yelled at him.

"Excuse me. Rebekka Franck, reporter at *Zeeland Times*."

He stopped and stared at me. He then approached.

"Rebekka Franck?"

"Yes."

Surprisingly he smiled at me.

"You don't remember me?"

I really didn't but wouldn't disappoint him. Besides, I really needed his comment for my article.

"Well, of course I do," I lied.

"Michael Oestergaard. You used to take dancing lessons at my aunt's dance studio. Jazz ballet."

"Miss Lejrskov's class. Michael. Oh yes, I do remember."

I really still didn't, but I remembered my dance teacher. Michael looked to be at least eight or nine years older than me. How could I have remembered him?

"Exactly. I used to hang out there with my brother and look at all the pretty girls. So you are a big-shot reporter now? I must admit I have been following your career. It has brought you around the world?"

"Sort of."

"And now it has brought you to Karrebaeksminde. I heard from the old Miss Jensen in the tourist-information-desk down on Gl. Brovej that you had come back."

"And she was right."

That woman did a little more than informing the tourists around here.

"So you work for the newspaper down here now?"

"Yes, I do."

"And you probably want a comment for your article?"

"I would love that." I was stunned. I couldn't believe his courtesy. Normally I wouldn't get a single word out of the police until they had a press conference, and then I would only get what all the other reporters got.

"Well, I can't say much." He lowered his voice and got closer. "But it ain't pretty, I can tell you that."

"But what can you tell me about what happened here. Is it a murder?"

"No doubt about it. Someone broke in through the back door and killed the guy."

"Do you have any suspects?"

"No, but we might begin with his wife," he laughed. "He wasn't exactly known as one of God's better children, if you know what I mean."

"I don't, I'm sorry. So you will be questioning the wife in the near future?"

"Sure, but don't write that. That would be interfering with investigative information. You know that."

"Then please just tell me what I can write."

"Write that the victim has been identified as Didrik Rosenfeldt, CEO and owner of the world-known company Seabas Windmills, and known as a part of the famous and very wealthy Rosenfeldt family. He apparently was killed by an intruder in his summer residence, there is an ongoing investigation, and that ... is it, I think."

I wrote everything he said in my notebook.

"Why hasn't the body been removed from the house yet?" I asked.

The detective sighed deeply.

"I really can't get into that."

Sune had probably been right.

"How did he die?"

The detective got an occupied look on his face.

"We don't know yet. That's for the crime lab to figure out. I am sorry but I really have to get on with my job ..."

"But surely you must have an idea?"

"We do, but we won't share it with the public, yet."

I nodded. That's what I expected. The crime scene must have been messy just as Sune said. I spotted Sune out of the corner of my eye. He took pictures of the body as it was finally removed from the house in a body bag and transported in an ambulance.

"Who found the body?" I asked Detective Oestergaard.

"The housekeeper found him this morning, when she came to clean the house."

"At what time?"

"She called us at six."

"Can we talk to her?"

"Well, I guess I can ask her."

I had to pinch my arm. I'd never met this kind of cooperation from the police. Were they always like this or was it because he knew me? Anyway, he left me for a second and came back with a small Philippine woman with an empty look in her eyes and an expression like she had seen the devil himself and lived to tell about it. It seemed she was still in shock and I knew I had to be careful.

I greeted her with a handshake and introduced myself. The detective left us, his duty calling. I waved at Sune and signaled I wanted him to come and take her picture. He came right away.

"So, that must have been real horrible for you," I began.

"I ... I just walked in, like I normally do. Normally he isn't in the house. I didn't expect ... I mean, how could I know?"

"Of course you didn't know. Can you tell me a little about what you saw?"

She didn't look at me but stared into open air.

"He was dead. Blood everywhere. On all the floors in the living room. All over the parquet. It was like a slaughter-house. He was shredded to pieces. Ripped apart like an animal would kill its prey. No man could have done this. Only a demon."

CHAPTER SIX

"**D**ID YOU write this article about my father?"

The chubby redhead man in front of me looked like his father back in the days when I used to see him down at the port hanging out and drinking with his boarding school buddies.

He had been waiting for me at the entrance when I arrived at the newspaper the very next morning. He held the paper with a picture of Didrik Rosenfeldt on the front page.

"Yes, I did." I opened the door into the editorial room.

Didrik Rosenfeldt Jr. followed me all the way to my desk.

"Can I help you, sir?" Sara said as she came out of the kitchen bearing a cup of coffee and a piece of cake on a plate.

"I want an apology from the newspaper. A formal one."

I looked at him. "For what?"

"For publishing this," he said and pointed at the interview with the housekeeper. "This line, where she says that a demon killed my father. Giving all kinds of details that the public shouldn't know about. I don't want you to write any more about this case. Do you understand?"

Sara placed a cup of coffee in front of me, and I took it.

"Did you want one too?" I asked.

He snorted and pointed at me with shaky finger.

"Do you know who I am, and what my family is capable of?"

"I think I might have an idea."

"I warn you ..."

"Or what?"

"Or ..."

I put down my coffee cup and leaned toward him. I wasn't afraid of anybody, least of all of him.

"Listen. You don't scare me one bit, mister. I have faced a lot worse bastards in my time in Iraq. And by the way, last time I checked we have freedom of speech in this country. Besides, they were the housekeeper's words, not mine. I just printed them. That is not illegal. So just fuck off."

I hadn't noticed Sune who had come in the room. Now I saw him smiling for the first time.

Didrik Rosenfeldt Jr. snorted again, very loudly this time, but soon realized that he was defeated. Blushing he turned around and walked quickly towards the door. Before he left he turned around and looked at me.

"This is not the last word in this case." He disappeared out of the room. I shook my head and sat down starting my computer.

"What a prick. Just like his father," I mumbled.

The two others in the room kept staring at me. Sara sat down and Sune started clapping.

"Way to go, Rebekka."

"It was nothing."

"Nothing? You just told the owner of the newspaper to fuck off."

I looked up. "He's the owner of the newspaper?"

"Well not directly. But his family owns the corporation that owns the newspaper."

I felt my body getting heavier in the seat. "So he could have me fired for doing that?"

Sune sat down at the corner of my table. "He probably wouldn't, I guess."

Sune looked at Sara.

"You'll be just fine," she said, not too reassuringly.

Moving through the day, I wanted to write a follow-up article about the murder. I couldn't stop wondering about the case. And I didn't want to. Now that I had risked my job and was probably going to get fired anyway, it didn't matter if I upset Didrik Rosenfeldt's son any more. I wanted to figure this case out.

A man like Didrik Rosenfeldt probably had a lot of enemies who wanted him dead. It could be for financial reasons. He was good for over $6.2 billion. That was 6.2 billion reasons to kill him right there. But he was also about to fire three thousand people in his company. That could have ticked someone off. He also had an investment company that may have made a bad investment for someone. Maybe he cheated someone for a lot of money.

And then there was the wife angle. He was known around town to be having affairs with a lot of women and bringing them to the summer residence. Maybe his wife simply had enough and she wanted him to suffer, to die a merciless death as revenge for humiliating her.

It had been seen before, but mostly in foreign countries. Denmark was a small country with only 5.5 million inhabitants. We didn't have that many killings or even that much crime compared with many other European countries. And almost every murder case was solved. Ninety-six percent of the cases to be exact according to the police department's own records.

I was very intrigued—and somewhat disgusted—by what the housekeeper said about the crime-scene and how the body looked when she arrived, and I wanted to know more. Maybe there was something in the way he died or in the way they found him that could tell me what kind of killer we were talking about. Could it have been a sex game that went wrong?

I picked up the phone and called my detective dance school friend at the police station, who was thrilled to hear from me, but he was of no help. They still hadn't gotten the autopsy report yet, so they didn't know exactly what had killed him.

Surprisingly, he ended the conversation by asking me out.

"Like a date?" I asked loudly.

Apparently it was so loud that Sara looked surprised at me with her headphones on. I smiled and pretended it was nothing, so Sara wouldn't spread the word. She was information central around here. No doubt about that. And I had to be very careful what I let her know about me if I didn't want the rest of the town to know it a few minutes later.

"I'm sorry, Michael. But I just got away from a bad marriage, and I need time to get back on my legs. And my daughter needs stability for now. But thanks. I'm flattered that you would ask." I tried to let him down politely.

"But maybe another time then?" He sounded so disappointed. I never liked rejecting someone.

"Maybe. Let's wait and see." I said goodbye and put the phone down.

So they didn't even know what killed the guy yet. Nothing new to put in the paper then.

I was beginning to get irritated and frustrated when I suddenly thought about my sister in Naestved. She used to date the Didrik and she and her friends hung out with him. I remembered how they hated him for not treating women well. My sister especially seemed to be angry with him after she dumped him. And it was more than just a normal hurt and anger after a breakup. She loathed him. Detested everything about him and his friends. Maybe I could make a sort of portrait of him.

I called headquarters and they loved the idea. So they hadn't spoken to Junior yet. Fine by me. I would continue. Go out with a bang. Didrik Rosenfeldt was a respected business man and well known in the jet-set society; he came from a noble family one of the few left. He was one step from royalty.

But he was also a prick, and I was going to tell the world the truth about him.

CHAPTER SEVEN

HENRIK **HOLCH** gave his credit card to the caterer. He had brought in the staff of the world famous Noma restaurant to cater the party. Everyone knew they had just won the world's best restaurant award last year. It had cost him a small fortune, but since he had a big one he hardly blinked when they gave him the bill.

"Just charge it to this card."

Long after they all were gone he could still taste the oysters and reindeer tongue with Jerusalem artichoke and marjoram along with the 2007 Chataeuneuf-Du-Pape "Les Vielles Vignes" from Domaine de Villeneuve Rhone-sud.

As always, his party had been a huge success. Now he needed some time alone, doing what he liked to do.

He crossed the living room with remains of the party everywhere. His housekeeper would take care of that in the morning, before his kids came for the weekend. Not that he particularly enjoyed their company. They had become annoying over the years, just like their mother. He laughed to himself, as he opened a bottle of whiskey and poured himself a large glass.

For now he preferred to be alone, without the fear that anyone might interrupt him and find out what he was doing. Some things were to be kept to one's self, like his father said once, when he walked in on Henrik masturbating in his room.

In order to get rid of the stench of cigars he opened the big French doors that led out in the garden. Outside his landscaper had made a beautiful play of lights for the guests to enjoy when they gazed out the windows. It was indeed beautiful. He unbuttoned his white shirt under the Armani tuxedo and took a deep breath of the cold fresh February air. Everything around him was proof of his success and power. Yes he had been somewhat of a party boy who wouldn't grow up, as his soon-to-be ex-wife called him. But so what? He deserved it. Yes he liked to do a little cocaine every once in a while, and yes he often had a few strippers attend the party and had sex with them afterwards.

So what?

He had always been like that. A real party boy. She knew that when she married him.

So what if he had turned 46 and still just played around? His wife's parents invented the shoes sold all over the world, and naturally he became the CEO of DECCO shoes when he was done with business school. Not that he ever spent as much time working as he did golfing and yachting and taking trips to Thailand. But wasn't life supposed to be lived? Who knew when it was over?

Henrik closed the French doors and went back into the living room and took the remote control and pushed a button. Then he turned off the lights with another remote. He was alone, finally. It was time for him to dedicate himself to his real pleasure.

Of course he did enjoy the company of all the Danish

actors and models and even occasionally the royal prince and his adorable wife. But to him they were all just faces and words to be forgotten. He wasn't a handsome man by nature but with a little plastic surgery over the years he had become quite attractive. With the fortune he was to inherit he had no problems getting women and sex whenever he wanted it.

But to Henrik, sex with a woman was strictly for the stupid. He enjoyed it, yes, very much, but it wasn't exactly a pleasure the way his trips to Thailand gave him pleasure. The way his movies gave him pleasure.

He opened the drawer that was locked by key and took out a DVD. He put it in the player and leaned back in the sofa. No, he certainly didn't know who those kids in the movies were. How could he? Or how they ended up doing what they did to each other and the adults in the movies. How should he know? Why should he care? People did all sorts of things for money. They even killed for money. Why shouldn't they be willing to have sex for money? All Henrik knew was that he paid a gigantic amount of money for it.

The Asian kid in the movie was giving an adult man a blow job and Henrik was just about to reach into his pants, dreaming that it was himself getting taken care of by the sweet children in Thailand, when he felt a violent blow to the head and, instead of pure sexual pleasure, felt nothing but pain in a sea of stars.

CHAPTER EIGHT

THE SONG. The song. He knew it, Henrik Holch thought to himself, halfway dreaming, and halfway getting back to reality. There it was again. He couldn't escape it. It sent chills down his neck.

"Three, four, better lock your door," someone hummed. Who was it? And why was it so hard for him to focus? He tried to move his arms but he couldn't. He squinted to regain his focus and see that figure standing in front of him, humming away. What was this? Why did his head hurt so badly? Finally he succeeded in opening his eyes and focusing, just to discover that he couldn't move. He was tied to a chair in the middle of his own living room. Tape covered his mouth.

In front of him a man sat in a chair, staring at him in silence. A brown briefcase sat on his lap. They stayed like that for what seemed like an eternity. He didn't recognize the man at first, but little by little memories came back to him. Some even overwhelmed him and brought tears to his eyes. Memories that had been blocked out of the brain by the alcohol and cocaine over the years. Memories that he was so certain he had escaped and never had to deal with again.

It gave him the chills to discover that he was wrong. Boy, was he wrong.

He wanted to ask what he wanted from him. Henrik wanted to offer him money to leave him alone and not rip up the past. *Some things are better kept to yourself*, he thought. There is no need to bring back that old story now. Why now? But he still couldn't talk and the man in front of him had decided not to.

The man continued to look at him in silence, and all Henrik could do was groan and moan. Moan over the past and all its cruelty. Moan over the future he was afraid he would never get.

And the man let him do it. He even looked like he enjoyed it.

Was that the purpose of all this? To make him moan? To make him regret and ask for forgiveness? If it was, he would do that in an instant. He would crawl on his knees and plead for mercy if it was necessary. And it would be sincere. Heartfelt. Because the fact was he really truly did feel badly about what they did back then. And he understood why he was about to pay for it.

Finally the man in front of him spoke. The sound of the voice again after all these years felt like needles ripping through his flesh.

"Hello, Henrik."

Henrik groaned behind the tape.

"Don't try to speak, because I won't understand a word anyway. And not to be rude, but I don't give a shit about what you have to say."

The man now opened the briefcase and took something out. Henrik's eyes grew wide. He tried to twist himself in the chair and get free from the wire tied him. But he had no luck. The man in front of him smiled while he put on the glove. Then he got up and went behind him. Henrik hyperventilated through his nose, while he tried to wring himself out of the chair.

"Nice house you've got here," he said and laid his hands on Henrik's shoulders. The four claws lay gently on the right one. Carefully he caressed his cheek with one of the claws.

"And you were about to watch a movie just when I disturbed you?" he said and looked at the big flat-screen on the wall, where he had paused the movie in a close up of the Asian boy with his lips closed around an old white man's dick. The boy's brown eyes were open and looked frightened.

The man put his lips close to Henrik's ears.

"You just got to the good part. I paused it so you wouldn't miss anything while you were out cold." He paused and stared at the screen.

"So that is still what you like. The younger the better, right? Isn't it so? And you have taken it even further than you did back then. They have gotten even younger. How old do you think this boy is? Six? Seven?"

Henrik didn't make a move or even a sound.

"You like that frightened look in his eyes, don't you? That's what turns you on, right? That's what used to turn you on back at the school. The fear painted all over their faces. And you were about to have some fun with yourself," he said and stepped around Henrik and now stood in front of him looking down at his crotch.

Henrik Holch looked down too and saw that his pants were still open.

The man reached down and took out his dick with his claws. Henrik Holch shuddered.

"See now you have that look in your eyes. That same look the little boy has," the man laughed. Then he leaned over and put his face next to Henrik's ear.

"Game over."

After that there was nothing left but Henrik's hysterical moaning, a muffled scream of pain from behind the tape.

CHAPTER NINE

S HE WAS so mad at him, she had not slept all night. All she could think about was the things she wanted to tell him, when she got hold of her husband. Once again he had let them down, and both kids were crying and didn't want to go to their dad's house for the weekend. It had become a habit of his to disappoint them and forget about them.

The night before they had a family party at the school. They were supposed to go, all four of them, as a family. As one unit. For the kids' sake. They weren't getting a divorce, she had told them. They were just living apart until they got their problems solved. That was the plan. They had gone to counseling together. Just the two of them and once with the kids. They were trying. At least the three of them were. It seemed Henrik wasn't doing anything to solve this. Again and again he let them down. He forgot to pick the kids up, he forgot all their appointments, and sometimes he would disappear for two or three days and she couldn't get hold of him. But she knew where he was. He was in the house or at the golf club, getting drunk and high and not answering the phone. And now she had found out that he had thrown a big party last night, when he was supposed to go to a family event at the kids' school. She had waited for him for two hours and then just taken the kids by herself. She had made excuses for him in front of the other parents.

"Henrik is just so busy lately with the company moving the factory to China and all. You know what it's like." She had laughed gently and the other women laughed back.

All big-shot husbands were busy and put the business before the family. That's just the way it is, they had all agreed.

She refused to give him the divorce he wanted. It wasn't acceptable in her family. They would work things out, or get separate bedrooms in the house and maybe they could be like her own parents, who just stopped talking and lived their separate lives. As long as they showed up to the right parties and charity events and were looking like a successful married couple who everybody envied, they were fine, and could do whatever they wanted once they were inside their own house again. Christ, their mansion was big enough for both of them to live there without ever having to have anything to do with each other again. They just didn't get a divorce.

"Not in our family," her mother had said, when she had cried her heart out in front of her and told her about her husband's increasing abuse of drugs and alcohol and the many trips to Thailand and strange videos he would sneak down to watch in the living room when he thought they were all sleeping.

"Learn to live with it; that's what we women do," her mother had snorted and made it very clear that this was not something she was to bring up again. She was supposed to deal with it.

Then she had begun to threaten him. The company he worked for belonged to her family. He would lose everything if they got a divorce. She would get the house, the kids— everything. But it didn't seem to frighten him one bit. He wanted out, he said. He wanted to go away for good. Move permanently to Thailand.

"To do what?" she had yelled desperately. "So you can pay young boys to give you pleasure all day? That's not love, Henrik. That's disgusting."

But he said he didn't care what she thought of him.

"I just want out of this marriage," he said.

But he was not going to get off that easily, she thought as she reached the driveway of her old home. The yard looked nice. The landscaper had done a nice job. She would remember to give him an extra bonus this month.

It was only six-thirty in the morning and she knew that it was time to take out the trash. She was going to put him in rehab. First she would take away his drinking habit, and then she would find some way to remove the other addiction that was destroying their life. She opened the front door with her key. The smell of cigars and strong alcohol hit her in the face. By the mess in the hall she could tell that a lot of people had been there. Probably models and actors as usual. Getting high, acting out, having sex in the bedrooms.

"Henrik?" she said out loud.

He was probably passed out in the living room as usual, she thought, and wondered how she would get his sorry ass out in the car. Maybe it wasn't too bad if he was passed out. Then he wouldn't be able to resist. She could just drag him out there. But she did bring her gun in her purse. Just in case. That would make him go willingly if he was awake. Or she could threaten to call the police on him. Whatever did the trick.

She never finished the thought, but froze in a scream when she saw the huge pile of blood.

CHAPTER TEN

I **SPENT** a couple of days researching the story, "Didrik Rosenfeldt's hidden past exposed." With a little help from my sister I had found out he and a couple of his friends were arrested in 1985, accused of having raped a local girl. My chances of finding the girl were slim. But Sune, our photographer stepped in. He told me he might be able to find the girl. He used to do "stuff like that." I told him to knock himself out and let him use my computer. It didn't take him long to find the girl's name and discover that she had gotten married and now had a new name, that she lived in Holme-Olstrup not very far from Karrebaeksminde.

The drive would only take eighteen minutes. I took Sune with me.

"So how did you know how to find her?"

He shrugged. "I just know a little about computers. I do stuff. Or I used to."

"Like a hacker?"

"You might call it that."

"Is that why you went to juvenile prison?"

He looked at me, surprised.

"Well I know a trick or two," I said. "Journalists can do things with a computer too. Like look people up and check their background. Or find somebody in the police who can."

Sune nodded. "Well it isn't like it's a secret. But yes, I used to hack myself into a lot of government stuff and one day I got arrested."

"How old were you?"

"Sixteen."

"So what happened?"

"I did my time. And when I got out I couldn't get a job anywhere. I made some bad friendships that weren't doing me any good. So I thought I had two choices. Either I stayed in Copenhagen and got into even more trouble with the law and became a real criminal or I get the hell out of there."

"And now you're supposed to stay away from hacking, right?"

He nodded. "They will never know I used your computer to find that girl's name."

"But you hacked in to the police database, right? And found the file from back then?"

"Yeah."

"So now I could get in trouble?"

"You won't."

I looked at him. He smiled.

"You have got a lot of confidence, don't you?" I said.

"Well, I am good. I don't leave any trace."

"Good. So why did you get caught when you were sixteen?"

"I was young and not careful. I know better now."

"So what happened to your fingers?" I asked and looked at his hand where he was missing the two fingers in the middle.

"Juvenile detention." He stared out the window. "I don't want to talk about it."

We had a long pause and reached the city limit of Holme-Olstrup.

"So, you never told me. What you are doing down here in the middle of nowhere?" Sune said, when I had parked the car.

I looked at him and opened my door. "The same as you are, I guess. Hiding from my past."

Holme-Olstrup is a town mostly known for its amusement park called Bonbon-land. It was born when a man named Michael Spangsberg, who was a candy maker, got the idea for candy with funny names: seagull droppings, dog farts, and pee diapers. The candy became so popular that many schools came to visit the factory located in Holme-Olstrup to see how the candy was made. But because of the hygiene requirements, the factory couldn't have visitors, so the founder decided to open a park, with a candy shop, a movie theater, and four boats in a pond. Today that had grown into one of the most visited parks in the country with more than sixty roller coasters and other attractions. It had put the city of Holme-Olstrup on the map.

I had been there once with Julie and her dad, when she was younger, and we were visiting my parents. I remembered the day and felt a little pinch in my heart. We used to be so good together. Better than all the others. We used to care for each other. Now he had ruined everything. How could I have been so blind? Love is blind, my dad would say. It was so true.

Irene Hansen opened the door. She was small and skinny with dyed blond hair. When I saw her face, I remembered her from back then. I just never knew her name. Her parents owned the shop at the port in Karrebaeksminde. We used to buy beer and cigarettes at their store on Friday nights when we were hanging out at the port doing nothing but meeting up with boys. She was my sister's age, about ten years older than me. I remembered her as a wild girl, always flirting with the boys, talking dirty, smoking and drinking. My sister told me the rape had changed her. After that her parents had been overly protective and never let her go out at night. They accused her of being promiscuous and said it was her own fault the boys raped her. If she hadn't been flirting this wouldn't have happened; if she didn't dress like a whore they wouldn't have done it. They had then dropped the charges against Didrik Rosenfeldt and his friends, but that only made everybody think the parents must have been right. She was to blame. Maybe she even led them on, and just regretted it afterwards when she faced the consequences. She got pregnant and had to have an abortion. My sister was one of the only people in the whole town who believed her story.

"Why?" I asked her.

"Because he tried to do the same to me," my sister said.

"What happened?"

"I went with him and his friends on his parents' boat one evening when we were still dating and he ..." she sighed before she continued. "He and his friends from the boarding school tried to rape me."

"Why have you never told me?"

"You were just a kid. I've tried to forget it ever since."

"How did you escape?"

"I jumped off the boat in time to get away. It was

summer so the water was warm and we weren't far from the coast, so I managed to swim all the way to the beach."

"Did you report it?"

"No."

That didn't seem like something my sister would do.

"Why not?" I asked.

"Dad convinced me that it would only mean trouble for the family."

I was so confused. That didn't seem like something dad would say. What had happened to him?

"Why?"

She sighed again.

"I don't know why. Please just forget about it, okay? There is no reason to be digging in the past now."

When Irene opened the door I saw a different girl than the one I remembered. This one was shy and timid. She looked at us with surprise. Normally I would have called first, but since this was a delicate matter I wanted to look her in the eyes when I asked her if she would give the interview for the article. I wanted her to see who I was and that I didn't mean to cause her any harm. I just wanted the people to know the truth. That's what I told her and she just stared at me in disbelief and shook her head.

"I don't want to talk about it," she said. "I'm sorry." She was about to close the door when I stopped her.

"Listen, Irene, I know this must be hard for you. But the guy is dead. Murdered. And a lot of people think the world of him. That he was a big-shot business man. And of course it is a tragedy that he was killed, but I want to tell the world what kind of man he really was."

"I'm sorry, but …"

"You can be anonymous, if you want. No one has to know that it was you."

She looked at me with mistrust.

"There is a lot you don't know about these kinds of people. They will know and come after me. Someone will."

"Please. Just let me hear your side of the story. Or Didrik Rosenfeldt will take it to the grave and you will never have your name cleared. Don't you want that?"

Irene was silent for a long time and I could sense she was debating within herself. Her mind was a battlefield right now, and I just hoped the right side would win.

After a few more seconds she stepped back into the house and opened the door and let us in. I smiled at Sune who smiled back.

Irene offered us coffee and we accepted. Sune was really polite and gave her a lot of nice compliments on the house and the décor. It wasn't something I would have thought he knew anything about but sometimes people just surprise you. And it was helpful. Getting to talk about something that interested her, she relaxed and got comfortable. Sune took some discreet pictures of her for the article, from the back and looking out the window. And by the time we got to the interview she seemed ready to talk. We all sat down.

"Tell me how it happened. How did you get to know Didrik Rosenfeldt?"

She sighed, preparing herself for the emotions and memories about to flush out of her like a big ocean wave.

"I had known Didrik and his friends from the boarding school for a long time. In the summertime when their school was closed, they always came down to Karrebaeksminde to stay at Didrik's house on the water or go sailing in his parents' boat. The parents were never there anyway and he and his friends were free to do what they wanted. And so they did."

"So they came in your parents' store at the port?"

"Yes, every time they went out on the boat, which was most days during the summer. They had to get supplies. Mostly cold beers and chips and stuff. So they came to my father's store and there I met them. Didrik always talked so nice to me, being a real gentleman. He knew how to talk to women. But he had his appearance against him, you know, he was a little chubby and ugly. So no one ever wanted to be with him. But I thought he was nice and had money and that attracted me."

"But the other boys had a lot of girls, I bet."

"Oh, yes. The boys always had girls with them out on the boat. And I always stared at them, jealous as I was. I remember that I really wanted to be one of the girls going with them out on the ocean, drinking, partying, and having a good time. I wanted to be one of the chosen ones. But I didn't come from a rich background as they did. I didn't go to boarding school, so I thought they would never take me."

"But they did?"

"Yes. One day. I was always flirting with Didrik because I knew he was the one making the decisions of who would go and who would not. Girls never really wanted to be his girl-friend. They would always choose one of the other boys. And that bothered him. So I chose him to be my ticket to have fun on the water. And one day, when they came into the shop to buy their beers, he asked me politely if I wanted to go with them and eat dinner on the boat and watch the sunset. I would be the only girl aboard. But that was meant as a compliment to me, he said. Because if they brought any other girl she would be jealous of my beauty. I was thrilled.

The one and only. I was to be treated like a queen and I could choose to kiss whoever I wanted of the rich boys."

Irene sighed deeply.

"I was so young and stupid."

"So what happened?"

"I got on the boat and the guys were so nice to me, like real gentlemen. I remember wearing a white summer dress and the wind was warm, unlike a normal Danish summer breeze. I was hot and we all cooled down with cold beers all afternoon. Admitted, I got a little dizzy from the beer and the heat. By dinnertime I was a little drunk, but not so much that I didn't know what I was doing. So I turned up the music and started dancing. The boys ate steaks and fish fillets they had brought from a restaurant on the port. We had champagne and real Russian caviar and I felt like I was in heaven, and then I just started dancing. The boys watched me and I closed my eyes for a second, enjoying the moment. When I opened my eyes I saw an expression on Didrik's face I had never seen before in any man. In any human being. He was like an animal getting ready to eat its prey. His nostrils were distended, and he breathed heavily. His eyes were filled with lust. And he was not the only one looking at me like that. All six boys were staring at me with that same look. The sun had begun to set, and the hunting was about to begin."

Irene shook her head and had tears in her eyes. I reached out and held her hand for awhile. I waited for her to be ready to speak again. I really didn't want to pressure her. After a few minutes she was ready again. I took a deep breath sensing that what was about to come would be very unpleasant. And I was right.

"They closed in on me. They got up and walked slowly towards me, smiling. I asked them if they wanted to dance, and they laughed. 'It's time to dance, all right,' one said and grabbed my wrist in an iron fist. It hurt. 'We will do the leading,' he whispered in my ear. I was scared and tried to pull away, but he held me and I suddenly felt a hand under my dress. Someone ripped off my panties and I started crying, pleading with them to let me go. Then they threw me to the deck of the yacht and took off my dress. They held my arms and legs. They were laughing and singing."

"What did they sing?"

She started humming. "That song from the horror movies popular back in the eighties. The one with the guy who had knives on his hands," she said.

"Freddy Krueger?" I remembered the movies. There were a lot of them as far as I knew. I wasn't allowed to watch them until I was older and by then they weren't that interesting anymore. But I remembered my sister talking about them and teasing me, telling me just before bedtime that Freddy Krueger would come in my dreams with his long claws and kill me.

"Exactly. They had a thing for that. They kept singing. 'One, two, he is coming' … And then he came."

"Who did?"

"Freddy."

"How is that?"

She shook her head and looked down. "One of them must have dressed up exactly like him. He was there in front of me. The same clothes, the red and black striped shirt, that brown hat and the glove, with the claws on the fingers. The person even wore a Freddy Krueger mask, so he looked exactly like him. I started to scream, and they said we were out in the ocean so no one would ever hear me. It was like they wanted to hear me scream. They encouraged me to do it. So I did. That was all I could do—cry and scream. They told me they would stab me with the claws, that they

would rip my body open. And then they cut me with them.
"

She lifted up her shirt. Long stripes of scars all over her chest were a constant reminder to her of that night of horror. She could never escape it.

"And then they raped me. All night. One at a time. They just kept going until I was numb."

Irene was quiet for a long period of time. I just stared at her and didn't know what to say. I'd never heard a story like this before. For a moment I thought about my daughter and wanted to lock her up until she was thirty. I tried to put myself in her parent's place but it was too unbearable.

"I must have passed out at some point," Irene continued, "because when I woke up I was lying in an old fishing boat at the port. I was bleeding everywhere. Some fishermen found me and called for an ambulance. I was at the hospital for four months."

I sighed and looked at her. She didn't indulge in self pity.

"I understand that you were pregnant?" I asked.

"Yes. The doctors discovered I was pregnant and removed it while I was still at the hospital. I haven't been able to have children since."

I nodded and thought again about my daughter. How fragile life was and how easy someone could just rip it apart.

"Then what did you do?"

"The police came to the hospital and took a report. I told them who had done it and what happened. They immediately arrested the six boys, including Didrik Rosenfeldt. But only a few hours later they were all freed. My parents told me they had dropped the charges against them. They had gotten a visit from a couple of the parents and received a big check for three million dollars. I was told never to talk about it again. My dad closed the store and we all moved away from Karrebaeksminde."

"That must have been difficult for you. That your parents dropped the charges without asking you?"

All of a sudden, I thought about my sister. Had they paid off my parents too? Was that why they refused to report the rape attempt to the police? I didn't like the thought.

Irene shook her head. "It was tough, yes, but I understood why. We would never stand a chance against the rich families in court. They would have the biggest, most expensive lawyers money could buy, and they would have won. Money can get you out of anything. They would find a way and we would be left with nothing but the shame. At least we got enough money that my parents never had to work again."

I nodded but felt everything inside me scream. What about the fact of trying to stop these guys from doing the same to someone else? Didn't that count for anything? Was money really that important? But of course I kept it to myself. I knew that to a lot of people in this world money meant everything.

Irene looked at me after wiping away a tear in her eye. "That's it. That's the story," she said.

I nodded again.

"I never saw them again, and hopefully never will."

I smiled and thought that while she had to live with the scars for the rest of her life, the boys from the boarding school continued their lives as if nothing had happened. That was the power of money. I was disgusted and more than ever I wanted to print the story in my paper. I wanted to disgrace Didrik Rosenfeldt's name and I didn't care what his son would say.

Irene interrupted my thoughts. "By the way, I actually

have a picture from that evening, "she said while she stood up and left the room. She returned after a little while with an old photograph in her hand. She handed it to me.

"Didrik took it just before we got on the boat. The camera had a timer on it, so we could all get in the picture."

I took the picture. It showed six boys in white and blue Lacoste polo shirts. They all smile with their arms around each other. And in the middle of them stood Irene in her white summer dress. Smiling with her bright white teeth. Off to have the time of her life. At least that's what she thought at the time.

"How did you get this?"

"Didrik sent it to me while I was still in the hospital."

What nerve that prick had.

"Can you please tell me their names, and can I borrow this?" I asked.

"Keep it."

W E GOT back at the newspaper about lunchtime and I sent Sune to a nearby café to get some sandwiches. I opened my computer and started typing when I sensed something was going on with Sara. She was so quiet, sitting there with her headphones on, just staring with an empty look in her eyes. I stood up and walked to her desk. She lifted a finger and put it over her lips to ask me to be quiet. She was definitely onto something. I waited a few seconds until she took off the headphones. She looked at me with excitement in her brown eyes.

"There has been one more," she said.

"Another murder?"

"Yes. The police are freaking out. They have never seen anything like this before, they keep saying."

I sat down on the corner of her desk. "I'll be damned ..."

"You can say that again. Looks like we've got ourselves a real serial killer."

I nodded speculatively. "Any names, yet?"

"Victim's name is Henrik Holch. Son-in-law of the

creators and owners of DECCO shoes. He was the CEO of the company."

I got up in a hurry and rushed over to my desk. In my bag I found the picture Irene had given me. I looked at the back where she had written the names of the six who raped her that night on the boat.

Henrik Holch was the last guy on the right. A slim blond boy with lots of pimples and a bright smile. And a bright future to go with it, I thought. I felt dizzy. I had actually found a connection between the two murders. So I picked up the phone and called Michael Oestergaard. He was busy, he said. But he would love to talk to me another time, just not right now.

"I have a connection between the two murders," I said.

He got quiet in the other end. "How do you even know there has been another murder? We haven't told the press yet. I just got here myself."

"Doesn't matter. The two murders are linked. They used to go to the same school. Herlufsholm boarding school. And they used to hang out together all summer. Down on Didrik Rosenfeldt's parents' boat. They were both accused of raping a girl in 1985 on that boat."

Michael was very quiet in the other end, and then he spoke with a little harshness in his voice. "Let us do the investigating, okay? I don't know where you get all that from, but we don't think the murders are related. They are too different in modus operandi, in the way the victims are killed. There doesn't seem to be any link between them according to our investigation. You are a reporter, so write that in your paper. Goodbye." He hung up.

I put the phone back in the cradle, stunned at his sudden change of attitude. Why didn't he want to see a connection between the murders?

Sune entered the editorial room with sandwiches. I explained everything to him while we ate.

"Maybe he's afraid you will write there's a serial killer on the loose, and that would create a lot of panic in the little town of Karrebaeksminde." Sune spoke with his mouth full and made me smile.

"You might be right. It would cause a lot of disturbance and anxiety among the locals."

"And keep the tourists away."

I nodded. He was right. Spring was on its way and with that came a lot of tourists and all the rich people living up north came to live in their summer residences. People came in their boats and ate fish on rye bread at the port, drinking beer and schnapps That was a big deal for the small town. A lot of businesses survived only because of them. It would be a disaster if they stayed away.

But inside of me the thoughts buzzed around. Who was killing the boys from the picture? Could it be Irene Hansen finally getting her revenge?

I wrote my article about Didrik Rosenfeldt, another one about the other murder of a high-profile businessman and a small story about who he was. I didn't mention the connection between the two killings I had discovered since I didn't want to scare the people and I certainly didn't want to make detective Michael Oestergaard mad at me. I needed a good contact at the police. That was worth a lot.

Sara had left me a note on my desk that Giovanni Marco had called three times while I was with Irene Hansen. I decided not to call him back. He probably just wanted to know when the article about him would be in the paper and frankly, with all that was going on, I didn't know when there would be room for it in the paper. I just told Sara if he called again to tell him we needed a picture of him and to make an appointment with Sune to go take it.

After that I went home early and spent the rest of the day with my beautiful daughter and my beloved old father. That was a very popular decision at home. We really enjoyed each other's company, playing games, talking, eating, and laughing. Julie said she had a great day at school, and that melted my worried heart. She had gotten a new friend in her class. His name was Tobias. While she told me everything about her new friend, I thanked God for my daughter. No matter how angry I was with her dad, he had given me her, and for that I was eternally grateful to him.

CHAPTER TWELVE

J ULIE HAD nightmares that night and she climbed in to my bed. I hugged her and lay close to her until she fell asleep again, but didn't get much sleep myself after that. My mind wandered.

I lay still in the bed looking at the ceiling just as I used to do as a kid. It hadn't changed. I knew every crack, every line in that ceiling and they were all still there. I smiled to myself, feeling happy about some things staying the same. And then I thought about the murder cases. I was excited about having found the connection. But how did I move on from here. Should I just let it go and let the police do the work, like detective Michael Oestergaard wanted me to? But how could I? I felt strangely attached to the case, and I knew something important. What if I could stop the killer from striking again? What if I could follow the investigation so closely I would be the only journalist to break the story about the first serial killer in Denmark? The thought excited me.

And I knew exactly how I was going to do it.

After dropping Julie off at her school the next morning I drove to the nearest furniture store before I drove to the newspaper. I bought a desk and a chair and brought it all with me in the car. Then I bought a laptop in another store and called Sune and asked him to meet me in front of the newspaper. When I arrived, he stood outside and was waving at me. I asked him to help me get it all up the stairs.

Inside in the editorial room we put the desk and chair down and unpacked it. It needed to be put together, so Sune helped me, while Sara looked at us in disbelief.

Finally when it was done we placed the desk next to mine and I smiled at Sune.

"Congratulations, this is your new workspace," I said to him.

He looked at me.

"What?"

"I want you to work with me on this case."

"How?"

"I need you to monitor the police work. Check the files, read the autopsy reports and so on."

His eyes were now big and wide. "Are you kidding me?"

"Nope."

"You want me to hack into the police's main server and look at their files. Are you insane?"

"I might be."

Sune sighed loudly.

"I would love to—you know I really love that stuff—but I can't ... I mean if the police caught me ... Once is one thing but several times makes the possibility of being caught so much bigger."

"How would they ever know? You said so yourself, that you were good at it, that you could do it without leaving a trace. I bought you a brand new laptop. It belongs to the paper, so we will all get in trouble if anyone found out."

Sune scratched his head. "I don't know..."

I suddenly felt bad pushing him into doing something illegal. I didn't want him to get in trouble because of me that was for sure.

"You know what? It was a bad idea." I closed the laptop. I sat down at my own desk. "Just forget it."

I opened my own laptop and checked my e-mails. Sune stood for a long time and stared at the empty desk. Then he sat down.

"Okay, but only on this case," he said. "Never again."

I smiled and handed him the laptop. "That's a promise."

It didn't take Sune long to find the autopsy reports of the two murders. He opened the files and showed it to me. Starting with Didrik Rosenfeldt's. It made me sick to my stomach. I was about to vomit when I saw the pictures of Didrik Rosenfeldt's body. The housekeeper had been right in her description. It did look like a wild beast had ripped his body apart. It didn't look like something a human being would be capable of doing. The body was almost unrecognizable. Only the red hair revealed it was Didrik Rosenfeldt.

I studied the pictures for awhile and Sune helped me, even though I could tell his stomach had a hard time too. It took us a little longer than it probably should have, but finally we looked at each other.

"Look at the cuts," I said and pointed at Didrik Rosenfeldt's chest.

"It looks exactly like ..." Sune said but stopped.

"I know. Like the ones on Irene Hansen's chest. Except these seem deeper."

"Exactly."

"What does that mean?"

Sune shook his head. "I don't know. Could it be the same guy, maybe? The same one who dressed up like Freddy Krueger and mutilated her body?"

"That sounds possible. But why? As far as her story goes they were all very good friends on that boat."

"I know."

"Let's look at Henrik Holch's file." I noted on a piece of paper the cause of Didrik Rosenfeldt's death was described in his file as death by stabbing.

With a few clicks Sune found the other file.

"This one is not much better," he said before opening it.

I nodded. I figured that.

The pictures on the screen were awful. But it didn't look like Didrik Rosenfeldt's or the cuts on Irene Hansen. That disappointed me. Maybe the police were right after all. Maybe there was no other connection between the two killings than the fact that they went to the same school. Could that really be a coincidence? I didn't believe it one bit. The killer had just changed his pattern. His modus operandi, as the police called it. Maybe he had a reason for doing it. I asked Sune to let me read the rest of the file and he found it for me.

Apparently the killer had cut off Henrik Holch's private parts, castrated him so to speak. And then he had left him tied up to a chair, bleeding to death.

I leaned back in the chair. What a way to leave this world. But why did the killer choose that exact way of killing Henrik Holch? Why not just rip his body like Didrik Rosenfeldt? Did he have a reason? I scrolled in the file and found my answer.

"Bingo," I said.

"What?" Sune looked at me.

"He was a pedophile."

"How do you know?"

I pointed at a line on the screen.

"He was killed while watching child porn on his flat-screen TV."

Sune looked impressed.

"So you think the killer chose a different way of killing Henrik Holch because he was into having sex with children?
"

"Yes."

"Like a punishment?"

"Something like that."

"So the first one was a bastard treating people poorly, having several affairs and just being a real prick all of his life, while the second one was a disgusting pedophile. Both of them had been involved in the rape of Irene Hansen."

"Exactly."

"So someone is actually doing the world a favor?"

"You can put it like that, yes."

I paused before continuing. "The question is, which asshole will be next?"

CHAPTER THIRTEEN

I N MY MIND, Irene Hansen could definitely be a suspect. She had the best motive for killing these guys, eliminating them one by one as revenge. But somehow I couldn't really see that skinny quiet woman being able to take down these men all by herself. Maybe she wasn't alone? She had a husband. Maybe he could have helped her. It was certainly a possibility.

My plan now was to find the rest of the men in the picture. To my surprise, headquarters loved my story about Didrik Rosenfeldt and wanted to run it in the morning paper. I expected to hear from Junior immediately after that. I cleared it with my editor and told him about the unpleasant visit the other day, but he said that I shouldn't be thinking about that. The Rosenfeldts did own the company that owned the newspaper, but they weren't supposed to be meddling in the editorial decisions. They had to go through him first, he said.

So I promised him another story about the six boarding school boys who raped Irene Hansen, a follow-up story to the first article. A "where are they now?" kind of article. I liked the idea. They raped a local girl, got away with it, and now they were living the sweet life of rich men.

"Make a small profile of each of them. The public will be interested in knowing who we have running around in our country, who they really are, especially since they all are very influential," my editor said.

So I was free to go after the boarding school boys.

I couldn't ask them about the rape. I had promised Irene not to blow her cover. She was hiding from them and told her story anonymously. But I could ask them about the two guys who were already dead.

It didn't take Sune long to find the first one, Ulrik Gyldenlove. He lived in Klampenborg in northern Zeeland, north of Copenhagen the richest part of the country. I called him and told him I was doing a story about two of his old friends from school. I wanted to talk to him about them, and much to my surprise, he agreed to meet with me.

We were to meet at Mattssons Riding Club next to Dyrehaven. It took about an hour and a half to get there. Dyrehaven was a famous area in Klampenborg. It was a big forest and had the richest animal wildlife in Denmark. It was famous for its many kinds of deer and especially for a big hunt that takes place every first Sunday in November. Hubertusjagten, as it was called, was an old traditional hunt that was more than a hundred years old. It was inspired by the old traditional English hunts in England, with the riders wearing red jackets using of fox hounds. Nowadays they didn't use the hounds any more or chase a real fox. Instead they had equipped two riders with a fox tail on the shoulder and then the rest of the riders were supposed to catch the tail.

The event was always broadcast on TV and people would flock to the park to see the hunt every year. Some of the riders always ended up in an especially muddy pond. People would gather around the pond in order to see who it would be this year who would end their hunt in a pile of mud, ruining the nice red jacket.

Ulrik Gyldenlove had just finished riding his horse for the day together with his daughter and they both got off when I approached them and told who I was. I told Sune to take some pictures of him with his beautiful horse and we chatted briefly with his twenty-year-old daughter before we went for a walk in the forest.

A fog was everywhere and it felt cold and damp on the skin. Between the trees I now and then spotted movement. I couldn't tell if it was a deer or another animal, but there was definitely something in there.

Ulrik Gyldenlove had only lost a bit of his hair since the picture was taken at the port. He had gotten older and wasn't as slim as back then. But I recognized the look in his eyes, and his smile when he now and then showed me one. He seemed burdened, as though life had been hard on him. That surprised me. I had expected him to be more like Didrik Rosenfeldt, caring more for himself than others. But this guy was different.

As we walked slowly along a path in the forest looking at the wildlife, he sighed deeply.

"This is my favorite spot in the whole world," he said and took in a deep breath of the moist air. "So quiet and calm."

I nodded. It was truly beautiful.

He looked at me with a smile.

"So how did you know I used to be friends with Didrik and Henrik? I haven't seen any of them in ages. We can hardly call each other friends anymore."

"Why haven't you seen each other for so long?" I asked deliberately avoiding answering his question.

"Oh, I don't know. It has been so many years. Time flies. We went to the same school for years and I have tried to watch everybody's careers from a distance, but we never saw each other since the day we graduated."

"Why do you think that is?"

He shook his head. "We were just school buddies. We really didn't have that much in common."

We walked down the path for awhile in silence. Then I took out Irene's picture from the pocket in my brown leather jacket. I showed it to him.

He stopped and stared at it for a long time.

"How did you get that picture?" He said.

"It doesn't matter. What does matter is that you seem to be much more than just school buddies in this picture."

He sighed deeply and put a hand to his forehead. He seemed a bit preoccupied for a second.

"What is it you want from me?" he asked.

"I want to know about your friends. What were they like? My sister used to date Didrik Rosenfeldt for a short while and she told me you and your friends acted out a lot when you came to Karrebaeksminde on summer vacation in the Rosenfeldt's residence. That you harassed people on the port area, and I know that you were at one point accused of having raped a girl on the boat."

Ulrik Gyldenlove sighed again.

"I just want to know the truth," I continued.

"You must do your research a little better next time," he said handing me the picture back. "The charges were all dropped. There was no case against us. They were false accusations. The poor girl must have been mentally ill or something."

"It was dropped because you paid her family off. Don't think I didn't do my research," I said, suddenly afraid of having said too much. Would they come after Irene for this?

He sighed again. "It's such a long time ago. Why dig up the past now? Why can't you just leave it alone?"

"Because someone is killing your old school buddies and it might be because of something you did back then. For all I know you might be next."

He looked at me with serious eyes. "Don't you think I have been asking myself that?"

CHAPTER FOURTEEN

ULRIK GYLDENLOVE was quiet for a long period of time while we were still walking on the path. I had borrowed a pair of Wellies at the Riding Club and they made a funny squelching sound when I walked. We reached Erimitageslottet, a small castle that never was used for the royalties to live in, but as a place for the king to have his banquet for the riders of the hunt. It was placed on the highest point of the forest overlooking all of the beautiful landscape.

It had a big history. I sensed that as we passed it.

"Most of the other students were afraid of that group," he said suddenly without looking at me. He stared out in the wide landscape that opened up between the trees. A flock of deer were gathered not far from us. One looked up and stared back at us.

"They enjoyed it. They liked to make people scared of them," he continued. "The school was their domain. And a lot of the other students got a taste of their tough love. They had a reputation of being like wild animals."

"What do you mean by they 'got a taste of their tough love'?"

"They beat them up. Sometimes half to death."

"Why?"

He looked at me. "For fun." He looked away again. "They got some kind of pleasure out of it. Sometimes there was no reason at all for them to pick on some poor kid and beat the crap out of him. He was just at the wrong place at the wrong time."

"I don't think I understand."

"What is there to understand? They were just pure evil. They wanted to be evil."

"But weren't they afraid to be kicked out of the school? Didn't their parents send them there to get a good education and a bright future?"

"You don't know a lot about boarding schools do you?"

"I'm sure I don't."

"Boarding schools are used for rich parents to get rid of their kids. Sending them to boarding school means they don't have to deal with them any longer. Most rich parents are emotionally inadequate, almost disabled. Because their own parents didn't love them, they are not capable of loving their children. Then they ship them off to boarding school and only have to spend time with them on the holidays. And even then they will be too busy for them. So they are left to themselves. Rich and merciless. Without any compassion for other human beings since they haven't gotten any growing up. That's the life of most boarding school kids. They did indeed want to amount to something. But they knew they would on account of their parents. And everybody knew if you wanted to be someone when school was over, you'd better not have pissed these guys off while you were in the school. If you were friends with Didrik Rosenfeldt you would surely amount to something later in life."

"But you are not like that. You are different, why?"

"I broke off with them in 1986. Told them I didn't want to be a part of their game anymore. It was over for me."

"Game?"

He sighed again. I sensed that he had been running from this story most of his adult life, thinking he could escape it, but now it had caught up on him.

"They had a game called 'A Gentleman Hunt.'"

"A Gentleman Hunt? What was that?

"It was a game that Didrik Rosenfeldt invented. One of the guys would come up with a fantasy and they would go out and make it real. Like raping the girl while dressed as Freddy Krueger. It was a challenge. Someone would challenge the rest of the group to do something awful and then they had to do it. If one refused they would be beaten up and thrown out of the game. To be excluded from the group meant no protection. You were certain to be their next victim."

"How did he come up with that?"

"One time he told us he had this fantasy about scaring the shit out of a boy in eighth grade, and then he told the rest of the group what he wanted to do to him, and then they all went out and did it."

"What did they do?"

"The kid was from the U.S. He had lost his parents in a car accident and had this one picture of them he always kept close to him, in his pocket. Didrik and the rest took the picture from him one afternoon in the boys' bathroom. They took it from his clothes while the kid was in the shower. When he came out all naked they showed him they had taken it. He wanted it back and started crying, but they didn't care. They stuck the picture in his mouth and lit it on fire. He was to hold it like that. If he dropped it they would shoot him, they said and placed a gun to the boy's head. As the picture burned the crying boy eventually burned himself and dropped the burning picture to the floor."

"Then what?"

"Then they pulled the trigger. But it clicked. It wasn't loaded."

"Wow. That was tough."

"The boy had to leave the school after that."

"What about Didrik Rosenfeldt and his gang?"

"Their parents paid the victim off and they continued their lives. And this was just the beginning. Now they started picking on all the new students who came to the school. Challenging each other in various fantasies and making them real."

"Someone must have been complaining about them to the headmaster."

"Some did every once in a while. And they paid the price for it. I remember one in particular who told on the boys and they hung him from the ceiling in the gym, by his arms. Then they beat him all night like a punching ball. He had to spend six months in the hospital. And he never told anyone who did it."

Ulrik looked up and spotted a falcon looking for food on the ground. He pointed at it and I saw it too. The fog had gotten lighter and we could now see more of the forest.

"Did they pick on you?" I asked.

"You only pick on someone who won't fight back."

I nodded.

"But I could have stopped them," he then said. "I should have."

We began to walk back to the riding club. I had promised

Sune I wouldn't take too long since we had a long drive home, and he had to pick up his son.

"You have a son?" I asked in surprise.

"Yes I do."

"You didn't tell me that."

"Well, you didn't ask."

His son was apparently seven years old. Sune was only nineteen when he got him. The boy's mother had been young too, and she didn't want the child. So he was a single dad.

I was stunned at the way people kept surprising me lately and wondered what else he had kept from me as we walked back in silence. I also wondered about this group of boarding school kids who had terrorized the whole school for years without any consequences. I wondered what role Ulrik Gyldenlove had in it and how I was supposed to put it all in an article without putting Irene Hansen's life at risk. I would have to discuss it with Ole, my editor, when we got back., We reached the riding club where Sune was waiting for us together with Ulrik's daughter.

"Can I see the picture again?" Ulrik asked just as we were about to leave.

I got it out of my pocket and handed it to him.

He stared at it and I saw sadness in his eyes.

"These two are dead now," he said and pointed at Didrik Rosenfeldt and Henrik Holch.

I nodded.

"Then there are only three of us left."

I looked surprised at him.

"You mean four, right?"

He put his finger on another boy's face in the photo.

"No. This guy, Bjorn Clausen, killed himself in 1987. That means there are only three left."

CHAPTER FIFTEEN

S O ONE of the boarding school boys was already dead. But how did he die? I searched the internet when we got back to Karrebaeksminde and in all the newspapers at the library. And I had Sune find anything he could on Bjorn Clausen and his suicide in 1987 from the Internet and the police archive. But all we got was a small note in the local paper and an old report from the police of what was a closed case, a definitely suicide.

Jumped out from a bridge in front of a train

I had run dry of ideas. Who was that guy? I asked myself and looked at the picture. Brown hair, blue eyes. Tall, muscular. He looked a bit familiar too me, but I couldn't quite place him.

I decided to let it go and concentrated on my article while Sune went to get his son. I told him he could drop his son off at my dad's and he would take care of him while we were working.

Sune called me after he had dropped off his son. I learned his son was Tobias, Julie's new best friend in school, so that turned out to be a very popular decision. I was getting quite good at this small-town life I asked Sune to bring pizza when he got back.

Jumping out from a bridge, getting hit by a train was certainly an effective way of killing yourself. But why? He was nineteen. He had just graduated from high school six months before. Was it just teenage depression? Ulrik Gyldenlove had described as a cold-hearted player of a game where they would beat the living out of kids that were younger than them and rape a local girl just for the fun of it Had he had some regrets? Some kind of conscience? Was he unable to keep on living knowing what he and his friends had done? It sounded a bit unlikely to me.

"Maybe the killer had already begun looking to get revenge back in 1987." Sune said with cheese from the pizza on his lip.

I signaled with my finger on my own lip, and he removed it.

"That's possible. But why wait twenty-four years before killing the next?"

"I don't know," Sune said with his mouth full.

"Maybe the killer has been away. Maybe he was sent to college somewhere out of the country. Maybe in England or in the U.S.?"

Sune nodded. "That sounds likely. A lot of these kids went on to become big-shots later in life and often they would have to go to foreign countries in order to get the best education money could buy before they came back and took over the family business."

"Exactly," I said.

"But that doesn't help us much," he said with a grin.

"What do you mean?"

"After what you told me today, almost every kid in that school could have a potential motive for killing them. A lot of kids were beaten and harassed and would like to get their revenge at some point."

"You're right," I said a heavily. "There could be hundreds of potential killers out there wanting to get rid of Didrik Rosenfeldt and his gang."

Sune took another piece of pizza from the box.

"So what do we do now?" He leaned back in his chair while eating.

"What is there to do?"

"Don't ask me."

"First I will write my article on the boarding school boys and where they are now. And then I will write another article on the harassment. I made a deal with Gyldenlove that I wouldn't use his name and thereby tell the rest of the gang he is the one who ratted them out. I will just call him an anonymous source from the school. Then I am going to e-mail the articles to my editor in Naestved. He is waiting for them and promised to read them right away and then put them in the paper."

"And then?"

"Then I will be going home to my family. My daughter is supposed be sound asleep by then, but since Tobias is there with her she will most likely be fully awake, running around having the time of her life. I will then tuck her in, after saying goodbye to you and Tobias."

"Then what do we do with the case?"

"What is there left to do but to wait for the killer to strike again?"

An hour or so later the door suddenly buzzed to the editorial room. Sune got up and let someone in. It was Giovanni Marco. He had come to get his picture taken for the article.

He had made the appointment with Sune since he was already in town doing some other business.

I smiled at him, and said hi, but didn't pay any more attention to him. I was busy with my articles. Sune asked him to stand against a wall and then he took a lot of different pictures of him.

Then they went outside to get some photos of him with some of his work displayed in town. Before they left Giovanni approached me.

I looked up and into his blue eyes. He smiled his handsome smile.

"I am sorry you threw away my phone number," he said with that cute irresistible Italian accent.

"Who said I threw it away?"

"I just figured, since you didn't call me back."

"Well, I didn't."

"Okay, then," he said and turned away.

"Okay."

He stopped himself and looked at me again. "Then maybe you would consider having dinner with me some day?"

I blushed and hoped he didn't notice.

"I might consider that."

"I will call you, then."

It was late when Sune and I got to my dad's home. Sune had been researching Bjorn Clausen for hours while I wrote the stories for the newspaper. The editor had read them and loved them right away. They would be in the morning paper, he said.

When we came inside we both had quite a scare. Inside in the living room stood two men twice the size of Sune. My dad was sitting on the couch looking at us with fear in his eyes.

"Dad, are you okay?" I yelled and ran across the room. I kneeled in front of him and looked him in the eyes.

He nodded and took my hand.

"I am fine, sweetheart. I am fine."

"Where are the kids?"

"They are upstairs. They are sleeping. Don't worry about them."

I breathed a sigh of relief and got back on my feet. I looked at the two guys staring at me and started yelling at them. "Who are you? And what the hell are you doing here?"

One of the men looked at me. "Peter sent us."

I froze. Sune looked at me. He grabbed my arm.

"Are you okay? Who is Peter?"

I looked at the tall bald guy with broad shoulders. I knew his type. He didn't scare me.

"Well then you can tell Peter to just butt out of my life. Out of our lives. I don't want anything to do with him ever again."

"Peter wants to see his daughter."

"Tell him I don't care. I don't want her to be among criminals. I want her to have an ordinary life of an ordinary girl."

I stepped a couple of steps in the big guy's direction while I kept yelling at him. The worst I could do right now was to show fear. Peter could never know that I was afraid of him. He would use it against me. Manipulate me into coming back.

I opened the door and showed the men out.

"You go tell him that."

CHAPTER SIXTEEN

"**Y**OU HAVE some explaining to do, young lady."

My dad stood by the stove in the kitchen the next morning when I came down. Julie had been sleeping when I woke up, so I let her sleep a little longer. After all, it was Saturday and she didn't have school.

I sat down at the table. I felt like I was thirteen years old again and my parents had caught me smoking.

"Can't it wait?" I said looking at my watch. I had promised Sune to go to the newspaper and look at the pictures he had taken of Giovanni Marco and choose three of them for the article about him.

My dad looked at me with discontent.

"I need to know. What happened to you two? You and Peter were so happy?"

I sighed. My dad poured me a cup of coffee and put it in front of me.

"It is really a long story, Dad ..."

He sat down with his own cup. "I have nothing but time."

I sighed again and took his hand. I smiled. How I loved

my talks with him when I was younger. I used to be able to tell him everything. He was nothing like my mom and sister who would always be so judgmental.

"You know we met in Iraq, right?"

My dad nodded.

"He was a soldier?"

"Actually he was an officer. I went there as a reporter and lived on the base. That's how we met. He took care of me, helped me get my stories for the paper, knew who I should talk to, and got me different interviews with the local people. I wasn't allowed to go anywhere on my own. That was way too dangerous, with all the kidnapping of foreign journalists going on at that time. So he his soldiers arranged to escort me everywhere I needed to go."

"And then you fell in love?"

"Yes. We grew fond of each other. He actually saved my life at one point."

My dad looked seriously at me. "You never told me that!"

"I didn't want to worry you."

"Well it's a little too late for that."

"I know. I never meant for you to be concerned."

"Then you shouldn't have gone to Iraq in the first place," he said with smile.

I smiled back and drank my coffee.

"Anyway, through my Iraqi interpreter I got promised an interview with one of the leaders of Al-Qaeda, a general high up in the hierarchy. It was a really big scoop for me. I had already become a big name from my previous articles about the war, but this one would put me over the top. My career would have been secured after that. But Peter wouldn't let me go. He said it was too dangerous because I had to go there alone without any protection."

"Well, of course, it was too dangerous. Are you kidding me? Did you really consider going?"

"I didn't just consider. I went. Without Peter's approval."

"You always were a stubborn little girl." Dad laughed, yet with obvious seriousness in his eyes.

"I know. No one could tell me what to do, right?"

"Right."

"Anyway, I went and of course it was a setup. There was no general there. Instead I got a black hood over my head and thrown into the backseat of a car. I kicked and screamed, but in a town like Bagdad, no one would hear, and if they did, no one would react."

"More coffee?" Dad stood up and poured us both a second cup. I could tell it was hard for him to hear this story.

"I felt the car moving and tried to listen to the sounds around me, trying to locate where we were going. I knew they would probably take me to the mountains and hide me in a house far away until my ransom was paid. That's what they usually did. But I also knew the chances of anyone paying the ransom were very small, since all nations participating in the war had agreed not to cave in to the pressure of terrorists. And then the kidnappers would probably have to kill me."

"Wow, I am glad I didn't hear about this until now," Dad said.

"Me too."

"So what happened? How did you get away?"

"The car didn't get far from the town when it crashed. I couldn't see what it was, but it felt big. I heard my kidnappers yell a lot but didn't understand a word, except the Arabic word for soldiers they kept yelling to each other. I sensed that hope wasn't all lost. I started yelling that I was in the car on the passenger seat and I heard the door open and someone dragged me out and took the black hood off me. It was Peter. They followed me anyway to the meeting with the alleged general and saw me being dragged out in the car. Then they crashed a van into the car carrying me and scared off the kidnappers."

My dad leaned back in the chair. "I always knew I liked the guy."

I smiled. Dad got up, got the toast and put it in front of me. I buttered it and put cheese on it. The way I always liked it.

Dad looked like he enjoyed watching me eat. He had a fried egg and poured a lot of salt on it.

"Easy on the salt there," I said. "I need you to stay alive for a little while."

"You are beginning to sound like your mother."

"That might be, but you had a stroke, remember? At the top of the stairs. The stroke didn't finish you off but you could easily have killed yourself falling down instead."

"That doesn't mean I can't eat salt. That just mean I should stay away from stairs," he said with a big smile and took a bite of the egg.

I laughed and ate.

"But you still haven't explained why things went wrong with you two," he said after a little while.

"Well, I got pregnant while we were still at the base and that complicated things. I told the paper and they sent me home. Peter came back after two months and we got married."

"That I remember. I am glad your mother got to see you in that white dress before she died. You looked so happy."

" I was."

"So what the hell happened to you?"

"I had the baby and everything was perfect until Peter had to go again."

"To Iraq?"

"Yes, he was deployed for another six months. When he got back something horrible had happened to him. I couldn't recognize him any longer. He screamed and cried at night. He got raging mad over small things and he couldn't take being home in boring little Denmark. It was like he didn't know how to live a normal life any longer."

"PTSD?"

"Something like that. I'm not sure, but he wasn't himself anymore. I couldn't rely on him. And he wouldn't talk to me about it. He cried when he thought I wasn't listening, he could get so mad he would throw things around and he even hit me a few times. Not hard, just slapped me a couple of times."

"He did not!"

"It's okay, I wasn't hurt, but I started speculating about Julie. Was this the kind of upbringing that I wanted for her?"

"So you came down here?"

"Not yet. First he went away again to Iraq. I pleaded and begged him to stay home but he said he had to go, that it was his duty. And I just gave up on him. I thought I at least would have six months of peace and a quiet normal life for me and Julie. And we did have almost a normal life for a couple of months until I found something. I hadn't heard from him in a long time so I wondered what he was up to. I opened his e-mail account and read all of his latest e-mails. I thought I would see letters from a woman or discover he was having an affair or something."

"But that wasn't what you found?"

"What I found made me so scared and so mad at him. It appeared that he wasn't in Iraq as a soldier in the Danish army. He had started his own private security company in Iraq with several of the soldiers from his battalion who had left the army with him."

"So, what was the problem?"

"Peter told me before about these so-called security companies. The name is just a cover up. They don't secure anything or keep anyone safe. They are mercenaries. They kill people for money."

My dad stopped eating and looked at me. "That can't be true. Peter wouldn't ...?

"Apparently he would."

"So what did you do?"

"I confronted him when he got back. And he didn't take it well. He locked me and Julie in the basement for a week. That was his answer. He didn't even defend himself."

"Oh my God, sweetheart," he said and held my hand.

"It's okay, Dad, don't worry. We're fine now, remember?"

"How did you get out?"

"Eventually he opened the door and let us out. We had to promise never to bring it up again or he would have to lock us again in the basement. I was really afraid of him after that and realized I couldn't live like this. He was a ticking bomb. So one day when I was supposed to be at work, I packed all I could and Julie and I came down here. The rest of the story you know."

My dad had a tear in the corner of his eye. I got up and gave him a hug.

"I'm so sorry I wasn't there for you. I thought you were just having the usual problems couples go through when they have kids. I'm so glad you came to me."

"Me too," I said still hugging him.

"What are you doing?" Julie had sneaked up on us in the kitchen.

I wiped a tear from my eye and let go of my dad.

"Nothing sweetheart. Grandpa is just so glad we are here," I said.

"So you started crying?"

"Well, yes. I missed him too, you know. Sometimes people get emotional."

She made an annoyed face and sat down at the table.

"Grownups are weird."

CHAPTER SEVENTEEN

LILLY, **THE** cat, sat on my bed while I was trying on dresses. I had spent a few hours at the newspaper with Sune, when Giovanni Marco called my cell phone and asked if I would have dinner with him at his house at the beach on Enoe. In my head I had a ton of excuses but finally I ended up accepting his invitation.

I suddenly envied the simplicity of the cat's life. Eating, sleeping, eating, licking herself clean. She just liked to relax, and take it easy with no complications in her life. Unlike me. This dinner could end up complicating my life even more than it already was, and I didn't exactly need that right now.

I finally headed downstairs wearing a purple dress that was a little tight but really showed off my figure. I was slim but not skinny. Ever since the pregnancy I still had yet to lose around five pounds that kept resisting my every effort to get rid of it. Not that it bothered me. I wasn't one of those women who got their self-esteem from the way they looked. And I had no idea how to go on a diet anyway. So I just made peace with it. But every now and then, like now, I missed my old body from before the pregnancy, when everything sat in its proper place. But by the look of my daughter and dad I could tell that I wasn't looking too bad.

"Wow, Mom! You look amazing. Very beautiful," my daughter said.

My dad smiled. "You'd better be careful with that man. He's a not a real man if he's not gonna try something to a stunning-looking woman like that."

"I will be very careful, don't worry," I said and kissed his cheek.

"Who is he? Tell me please who he is," Julie begged me.

I kissed her on the cheek too.

"Later, sweetheart. It ' nothing but a dinner with a nice man I met through work. That's all it is."

"But why are you eating with him? What about Dad?"

The question I had dreaded. I was squatting in front of her looking her directly in the eyes.

"It is just a dinner. I promise you that."

"Okay."

I kissed her again and got up. "Do I look all right?"

"You are so beautiful, Mom."

"Thanks."

I knew I could trust her. Her eyes were like a mirror of truth. She would not hold back if she thought I looked horrible.

"Don't wait up," I said and left the house as they waved at me.

I drove there since I had no intention of drinking and losing control. As I pulled into the driveway of the beach house, I almost regretted my decision. I had just split up with my husband and I wasn't emotionally ready for anything new yet. And neither was Julie. She didn't need a new man in her life right now.

But then, I really liked the guy. Yes, he was a little too much into himself and his artistic work, but there was something incredibly sweet about him. And he had a way of being a real gentleman with me. He always held the door, a virtue a lot of Danish men had forgotten all about. He listened when I talked and he would actually remember what I said afterwards. I thought, *Maybe I just need to have someone spoil me for once* and went up to the door.

I got to be spoiled all right. Barely had I sat my foot in his beach house before he placed me on the floor in a pile of huge pillows with a glass of red wine. Italian of course, my favorite. Then he prepared dinner for us. Barefoot, of course. I drank some of the wine saving the rest for the dinner since I could only have one glass if I was to drive home. And that was still my intention.

Dinner was amazing. He had set the table with candles and fresh flowers. And then he served the food.

"Tomatoes with balsámico vinegar di Módena, and buffalo mozzarella," he said in Italian and sat down in front of me. He wore a white shirt. The two top buttons were opened and I spotted a gold cross on a chain underneath. He was probably Catholic.

"Dig in."

I lifted my glass in a toast. "To *le chef.*"

He smiled and we drank. As we started eating he looked at me.

"What?"

"Nothing I just really like to watch you eat my food. You are not one of those women who won't eat."

"I am not, no," I said with my mouth full. "I love food.

You won't be seeing me not being able to finish my salad and water."

He laughed.

"Well I'm glad. Because the next dish is Rigatoni al Tartufo. And that is not for people who are afraid of a little butter and fat."

I smiled.

"What is it?"

"Rigatoni with tenderloin, truffles, and chanterelles."

My mouth was watering just by the very thought. "Bring it on."

Of course I couldn't just have one glass of that wonderful red wine, so when he offered me a second, I decided I would take a taxi home. Then I could enjoy the evening without having to think about drinking and driving. So I had one more glass, and a few more after that. After dinner we sat on the pillows on the floor and he lit a fire in the fireplace. The beach and ocean were all black outside the big windows and it felt like looking right into nothingness.

"Do you want to feel the ocean breeze?" he asked.

"I would love to."

He put on a sweater and I took my big winter jacket and then he opened the door to the porch and took my hand. The wind was freezing. It felt like it was biting my cheeks. I took in a breath of the fresh air.

"I just love this place," he said and looked out over the ocean.

I did too, I had to admit.

"Come let's go all the way down to the ocean," he said all of a sudden while pulling my hand.

Like a schoolgirl I followed him. We ran to keep warm.

When we got there he stopped. The half moon rose over the water. Without a warning Giovanni just grabbed me, pulled me near and kissed me.

CHAPTER EIGHTEEN

I **WOKE** up with the worst hangover in history. At least for me, that is. Not only did I have too much of that great Italian wine the night before, but I also woke up in Giovanni's bed. Something I had promised myself wouldn't happen. So the regrets were hurting more than the actual headache.

What had I done? What the hell was I thinking? Who is this guy anyway? I didn't know anything about him and now I had slept with him. And what about Julie? She might have had a nightmare and tried to find me in my bed, but I wasn't there. Who would have comforted her?

I sat up in the bed. I was naked. My clothes were on the floor. Giovanni was still sleeping. It was only five thirty in the morning. I could hurry home and pretend like I had been home all night. It was not impossible.

I hurried and collected all my stuff and sneaked out. I felt like an idiot from some movie but this was how I wanted to deal with this for now. I had to get away.

Julie was still sleeping in her bed when I got back to the

house half an hour later. Quietly I sneaked into my own bed and got under the comforter. I even fell asleep for half an hour more before she woke me up.

She stood beside my bed. Her arms were crossed in front of her chest. I sat up.

"Morning, sweetheart. Did you sleep well?"

"Where have you been?"

Oh, oh.

"Come sit," I said and padded on the bed.

She sat down.

"I slept at that man's house. It was too late for me to drive all the way home."

"But you promised that it would only be dinner."

"I know. But we were having a real nice time. He is really nice to talk to. And then I forgot about the time."

"I sure wish you didn't."

"I know."

"What about Dad, then? Who is going to eat with him now?"

I sighed. She was always so direct. "I don't know. I really don't know, sweetie."

"Why are you still so mad at him? He said he was sorry for locking us in that basement."

"But he also said he would do it again if we didn't do as he told us to. I can't live like that. You'll understand when you get older. I'll explain it then."

She reached out and took my hand. "I understand it now, Mommy. I don't wanna go back in that basement either."

I smiled.

"Come here and kiss me, peaches," I said and tried to grab her.

She laughed and screamed and ran out of the room. "Try to catch me if you can."

Giovanni called a little later when we were in the middle of a big puzzle on the floor. All three of us were heavily concentrating on the project.

"You were gone when I woke up," he said with a gentle voice.

"I know, I'm sorry."

"No note or anything? That was brutal."

"I know. Sorry. I just needed to get back to my daughter."

"I understand. I just never had a woman sneak out on me before."

I laughed. "Well, there's a first for everything."

"It's quite intriguing I must say. It makes you mysterious and hard to get. I like that."

I laughed again. "I'm glad you do. 'Cause I really had a nice time last night."

"Me too. Let's do it again, then?"

"Let's do that."

PASTOR **B**ERTEL Due-Lauritzen was a holy man. He knew God and had a personal relationship with him. Everything he did was directed by the Lord himself. At least that is was he told himself when he hung up his collar at the end of the day. The kids in the juvenile detention center where he worked called him the Bishop which he didn't mind too much since he knew all are created equal in God's eyes. And like a bishop, he worked for God. He was there to tell the juvenile criminals about God, that there was a way out for them and his name is Jesus. It wasn't too late for them to change.

In the very beginning when he first came to the detention center, he had been very patient with the youngsters. Since it was a prison, he had made what he called a confessional chair in the prison church even though he wasn't Catholic. But he found it useful for the kids to be able to talk to him anonymously about what they had done. What he didn't tell them was that he would always know who it was on the other side of the curtain he had put up.

When they came to confess their sins, he would nod

and ask them to repent and ask for forgiveness and then they would be off to do more damage. But they seemed to keep on getting themselves into trouble. Again and again he had to ask for God's forgiveness in their lives, but nothing seemed to change. And he had a difficult time coping with the teasing behind his back. They would laugh at him when he gave them a Bible to read or when he would give them a Bible quote he thought might get them through the day.

"Remember you are all children of God. He will forgive you and love you if you ask him to," he would say. But they wouldn't listen. No one would.

He had given up on his old lifestyle. He had to. Give up his rich and wild life where everything was possible. Where the cars were big and the boats even bigger. After boarding school, he told his parents he didn't want to work for their company. He didn't want to end up like them. He told them he was gay and wanted them to accept it.

They had slammed the door right in his face. Called him a disgusting faggot and told him they never wanted to see him again. He was no longer their son.

After that he had to get by without his parent's money for the first time in his life. He found love and helping hands at the gay bars of Copenhagen. Men brought him home and gave him money to have sex with them and sometimes he even got to spend the night. He lived on the streets, selling his body to whoever wanted it, eating only whenever one of his clients was kind enough to buy him something at a bakery or a hotdog stand. And he thought he had deserved that life. He loathed himself. He hated that his sexuality had brought him into this mess. Why couldn't he just have oppressed it? Why did he have to blurt it all out in front of his parents?

One day he had sex in an alley with a man who turned out to be a priest. He proved to be a really nice guy and they started talking afterwards. He told him he had known ever since he was a kid that he liked men. But he had learned not to express his sexuality in public.

"As a priest, no one would ever ask you why you don't have a wife and kids," he said. That gave Bertel an idea. Not only could he hide his ugly disgusting, impure thoughts from the world, maybe he would also be able to help someone else out of their miserable lives. Maybe even young kids who needed to be saved, as he had needed it, when God came along in form of a priest.

After getting an education, with a little help from his friend from the alley, he got a job working at the juvenile detention. But very soon he realized he didn't make much difference in their lives. He reached out to them but they didn't change. God didn't work in them and make them better. So he went to his altar and prayed about it.

"Why won't they change, God?" he asked. "Why do they keep laughing at me? Why won't they listen to your words?"

And he had gotten his answer. In God's own words. "So if your eye—even your good eye—causes you to lust, gouge it out and throw it away. It is better for you to lose one part of your body than for your whole body to be thrown into hell. And if your hand—even your stronger hand—causes you to sin, cut it off and throw it away."

Jesus had said it like that. So it had to be, then.

Pastor Bertel had then gone to one of the kids in the middle of the night and put acid in both of his eyes. Of course, he had sedated the kid first. He wasn't a monster. And then he had left him there for someone else to find. No one ever knew how it happened but the kid never looked at a woman with lust again. And he never raped anyone again.

That's how he began his real work for God.

Sometimes he would just teach the kids a lesson by beating them senseless and threatening them with death if they told anyone, and sometimes he had to go to more extreme methods in order to reach the youngsters. Sometimes he had to castrate someone to keep him from raping.

After a while, it had become even better than back at the boarding school when he and his friends used to beat other kids up, because this wasn't meaningless. This was to make someone's life better; this was working for God. And in the end, when it was all over, all that would matter was what he had done for him during his time on earth.

CHAPTER TWENTY

PASTOR **BERTEL** Due-Lauritzen had just ended his ten o'clock Sunday service As usual, he would tell the juvenile criminals to come to the confession chair afterwards and tell him their sins. Now he was sitting in his chair waiting for someone to show up on the other side of the curtain. He waited for a long time, but knew nothing would happen. Pastor Bertel sighed deeply. It was always the same.

In the calm of the prison church that day in February he thought about the summers of years past. The smell of the sea, the laughter, sailing in the open water with his friends, the look on Bjorn's face just before he jumped with the other boys in the water naked. Sitting on the deck wanting to kiss Bjorn and touch his soft skin. The lost desires in the light summer night. The unfulfilled longings. The torture of being so close to someone you love and not being able to express your emotions. Because he knew they would have resented him for it. They would have hated him if they knew how he felt.

And Bjorn would have been the worst. He would have hated Bertel more than any. Bjorn always was the strongest among them. He was the one with all the ideas. He came up with the Freddy Krueger rape. He even made that glove himself. He could do stuff like that.

Bjorn wasn't quite like the average boy on the boarding school. He wasn't rich and he could make things with his hands. If they ever were deserted on a desert island he would have been the only survivor. Not because he could have build a hut or caught food, but because he would have killed the others and eaten them. He was like that. He was a beast. The evilest among them. And Bertel had loved him. He had loved his strong muscular arms and his beautiful strong face. He had even loved the beast inside of him.

And then Bjorn killed himself.

A few months after their graduation he jumped off a bridge and was hit by a train. Bertel could never understand why he would do such a thing. It was incomprehensible. He had cried for days when he heard it. That was when he had decided to tell his parents the truth about himself. He couldn't hide it any longer. At least that is what he thought.

Boy, had he been young and naïve.

Bertel touched the rough fabric on the armchair and thought about the few times he would reach out and touch the skin on Bjorn's arm without him knowing why.

Suddenly, he felt the solitude was broken, that he was not alone in the church. A light step, almost noiseless moving across the floor. Then calm, regular breathing behind the curtain. Pastor Bertel waited for the person behind the curtain to be ready. He looked under the curtain and saw the shoes, as he would always do. He would memorize anything he could about them. Their color and shape or even brand. Then he would later find them in the dining hall and know the face of the owner. But these shoes were different than the ones he normally saw under the heavy red curtain. Mostly the youngsters wore sneakers or Converse. But these were shoes like the ones Bertel would wear. Like a man of his own age would wear.

Bertel smelled the perfume of clean skin mixed with good cologne. And all of a sudden he recognized the smell. That exact cologne that only his long lost love would wear.. Bertel widened his eyes at the sound of the song long forgotten.

"Five, six, grab your crucifix ..."

"Who are you?"

A moment of silence, and then the man answered in a deep resonant voice. "Does it matter?"

"Yes it does."

"Who I am is of no importance."

"Then what is important?"

"Why I am here."

Pastor Bertel felt his throat constrict. The feeling of suffocation overwhelmed him. "I have read about you in the paper. You killed Didrik and Henrik. I figured you would come for me too. In a way I have been waiting for you."

Bertel had an urge to get up and pull away the curtain to see his perpetrator's face. But something kept him from doing it. Some force bigger than himself forced him to stay in his chair. The same force that the boys in the juvenile prison had come to know after the nightly visits with the prison's pastor. The same force that would keep them awake night after night staring anxiously at the door to their cell. Afraid that it would open and they would once again lose a finger, an ear, be blinded, or even castrated.

It was fear.

"I suppose there's nothing I can do or say to make you change your mind?"

"You suppose right."

"So it is over?"

A long motionless silence. For an instant the pastor in the armchair thought the man behind the curtain was gone.

"Can I please at least see your face?"

Another silence from his perpetrator before the sound of the curtain being pulled aside filled the air. A face appeared on the other side. The glove from his past was pointing right at him. The pastor wasn't afraid any longer. But he was indeed surprised.

"So it is you?"

"Yes."

"But why? Why now after all these years?"

"Because your time is up. The game is over."

The pastor was content with the answer. He had always known that the past that he had too long been running from, would one day catch up with him.

And this was it. His time was up. After all he was a priest. He wasn't frightened by the end, only by the pain.

"Will I suffer?"

"Yes."

End of Excerpt

———

ORDER YOUR COPY TODAY!

GO HERE TO ORDER:

http://amzn.to/2vmp78f

Made in the USA
Middletown, DE
10 May 2021